A colle

The Nutcracker Nibbles Christmas Case by Jeanne Kern

Death by Gingerbread Drops by Jo A Hiestand

Snow Kiss Cookies To Die For by Wendy Kendall

Sprinkle With Sugar

by

Jeanne Kern
Jo A Hiestand
Wendy Kendall

This is a work of fiction. Names, characters, places, and incidents are either the product of the author's imagination or are used fictitiously, and any resemblance to actual persons living or dead, business establishments, events, or locales, is entirely coincidental.

Sprinkle With Sugar

The Wild Rose Press, Inc.
PO Box 708
Adams Basin, NY 14410-0708
Visit us at www.thewildrosepress.com

Publishing History
First Edition, 2022
Trade Paperback ISBN 978-1-5092-4494-2

Published in the United States of America

The Nutcracker Nibbles Christmas Case

by

Jeanne Kern

Christmas Cookies

Dedication

to John Dickson Carr,
the king of the locked room mystery

Chief Julia Dunnigan and her team stared glumly at the murder board. Seven DMV photographs hung from pins, faces staring blankly into space. In the Victim space, the studio-created book jacket portrait of the deceased, Walt Sheridan, beamed benevolently down.

Walt Sheridan—everyone's Grandpa. The beloved author of a family saga. Each new book an instant best-seller. Television series for years. And the world knew Walt Sheridan himself as the model for the family patriarch everyone wished were his own grandpa.

Now dead.

Dead in a locked room with no weapon.

"It shoulda been a simple suicide," a bass voice muttered. Nobody looked to see who spoke. Nobody had to. Lieutenant Phil Riley was gruff, grumpy, and usually gloomy.

Yet there was something about him. Julia had felt it her first day on the job six months ago. He was far from handsome, but her one unhappy marriage had taught her that looks didn't matter. Commitment. Staying the distance. The stability of age. That was important. And Phil Riley had obviously stayed the distance. Twenty-six years on the force and counting.

He'd been the obvious choice for promotion to the job of Chief. When the town council brought Dunnigan in from a neighboring state, Riley took it personally and undermined her at every turn. She'd had to prove herself over and over to gain respect and maintain authority.

Well, nothing new about that. She was a woman in a man's world. It went with the territory.

She was efficient. A people person. A hard worker. And she didn't take offense at Lieutenant Riley's grumbling and carping. Not only had she not bitten back at Riley's antagonism, she'd laughed at his ill-humor.

Well, she couldn't help it, really. He was so over the top with grump, giggles just bubbled up inside her whenever he complained. In fact, giggles weren't the only thing bubbling up in her. After two weeks of squaring off with Riley, Julia had to admit he made her knees weak, her palms sweat, and all the other clichés of a teenage crush.

Once she realized this, Julia pored over the policy books. No non-fraternization mentioned. And the head of the Robbery Division was married to one of his officers. In this community, she was told, couples frequently worked in the same place—it increased stability. Not that it mattered. Riley had only warmed from Actively Antagonistic to the bottom of the Cool Acceptance scale.

Her laughter had startled him at first. But it pleased him, too, she could tell. And her work ethic had won him over. She knew her business, and she had a keen mind for crime.

Until now.

She turned her attention to her crew. "Any new thoughts? Lieutenant Riley?"

"I think the wife did it. It's always the wife." His gruff voice brooked no argument. He got one anyway.

"But she was in the kitchen setting up the menus with the cook," Sergeant Edgars said. "I like the son for it. He was always asking the old man for money. Maybe this time he didn't get any and he snapped."

"But the son was helping the secretary move boxes of files from the office to the basement. The valet and the maid were together upstairs." Freddie, the young tech expert, added, "We've been over that. Everyone can give an alibi for someone else. The cook and the wife were together. The son and the secretary were together. Of course," he continued, "there aren't any security cameras."

"So we have to take their word for who was where," Officer Sykes offered. "And what about Sheridan's neighbor, that Mr. Forrest? He just showed up alone. And without any reason."

Chief Dunnigan shook her head. "He had a reason. He was bringing his friend a Christmas present. When everyone but Sheridan convened for lunch, the wife invited him to stay. Everyone is a suspect. The problem isn't finding suspects. Or motives. The problem is the weapon. We don't have one."

Another silence fell. The old clock clacked and the minute hand hopped forward. Since the clock's hands registered a change only once every five minutes, the clock served no purpose as a timekeeper, but it had always been on the wall, and the police squad almost never even heard the whirr and clack. This time Julia used it to energize a slow rise to her feet.

"Look. One more time over the case, and then we have to free our minds and get out of our ruts. So. Walt Sheridan, beloved author of a best-selling family saga…"

"Soon to be a major motion picture," Lt. Riley inserted.

"Right. Big money-maker." Julia flashed a smile at Riley. No accounting for attraction, but his deep voice always made her tingle. He showed no signs of reciprocation.

Yet, she reminded herself.

"And having finished the new book at about ten a.m., according to all witnesses, Sheridan called his family together—apparently a ceremonial tradition—and they counted down to one, when he hit Send on the secretary's laptop, and off it went on its way to being yet another Sheridan financial and emotional triumph. They lifted a glass of...um..." She looked at the ceiling for a beat before she went on. "Cranberry juice, and drank a toast together. Then Sheridan shooed them all out so he could begin the next project before he 'went cold.' He always tried to get the first two pages of the next book or script on paper—apparently hunting and pecking on his old Royal typewriter—before he left the room. Again, quirky, but normal."

Julia began to pace. "While the wife, the secretary, the son, the valet, the maid, and the cook were in the house, Sheridan took a bullet to the right temple and died instantly. All windows and the door to the study were locked. Nobody heard the shot. The body was discovered only after the son broke down the door when Sheridan didn't respond to the bell for lunch." Julia took a deep breath, rolled her shoulders to loosen her tension, and went on.

"The secretary called us in. Immediately, she said. There was no weapon to be found. So. A locked room death. Suicide the obvious solution, but there is no gun. Everyone has a witness to his or her whereabouts prior to the discovery of the body. And they all remained in the living room until we arrived. Or so they all say," she added, nodding at Officer Sykes. "So. Where's the gun?"

She threw her arms up in temporary surrender. "I

don't know about you, but my head hurts. "It can't be suicide because—no weapon. It can't be murder because—locked room. So somebody or everybody knows something he's not telling."

"It's always the wife. Like I said." Riley glared around the room, demanding confirmation.

"Thank you, Lieutenant Riley. But we do have to have some proof. Look. All our suspects are confined to the conference room. They're all together, but they were all together before we arrived on the scene. They're having lunch, and we've stationed a patrol officer with them to note anything of interest any of them might say. I suggest we go home, eat something, take our minds off this case, and try to relax. Maybe one of us will have a Eureka Moment. Back in an hour. Except you, Freddie. You get busy running down the financials. And Edgars, on your way, pay a visit to the attorney. See if you can find out who gains the most from Sheridan's death."

Outside, Chief Dunnigan inhaled the bracing December air and exhaled the always-stale aromas of the squad room. Why did it continue to smell like damp cement, old smoke, and wet dog? She'd scrubbed it many times, hung air fresheners, even burned sage to dispel the odor, but nothing seemed to work. Maybe that was just what old sins smelled like.

But she didn't have to breathe that now. She was heading home to bake, to fill her home with the scents of cinnamon, vanilla, sugar. All the favorite smells of the season, aside from pine needles and candle wax. After all, it was Christmastime. Baking cookies was almost a law.

Well, she didn't have time to do the baking now, but she could put the dough together and refrigerate it. She'd make the filling and bake when she got home for the night. Bringing cookies to the squad room tomorrow morning might give their bodies energy and their brains a sugar boost.

In fact, it had been her bakery goods that won over several of her squad from the beginning. But not Phil Riley. He pretended disdain at her sugary offerings. But he surreptitiously filled his pockets. When Julia saw that in the corner of her eye, oven-warmth encompassed her. Riley was a tough nut, but that shell would crack. She could wait.

But this death could not.

And that was the toughest nut of all. The shell of the sealed door. The shell sealing out easy answers. So many nuts to crack.

Her brain took a sudden turn. Nutcracker! She'd bake her Nutcracker Nibble cookies. They certainly fit the crime. And they fit the season. As a child, Julia had helped her mother make them every Christmas just before they went to *The Nutcracker* to watch the dancers present that timeless story.

Turning onto Oak Avenue, where there wasn't an oak to be found, usually tickled Julia. But not today. Even now, the news was spreading beyond the local. Sheridan was America's Grandpa, and America demanded answers.

Today she too wanted answers. And back went her one-track brain to the uncrackable nut of this case.

The squad had arrived at the Sheridan manor at sixteen minutes after one o'clock. A small ping of satisfaction for such a prompt answer to the secretary's summons didn't last long. The maid opened the door and, mouse-like, ducked her head and led them into the living room.

Julia expected a warm, colorful, and welcoming room, one where children would feel at home to play and grownups could sit comfortably in smaller conversation areas. Featured, she knew, would be the outsized rocking chair from which Sheridan dispensed wisdom, kindness, and peppermints, just like the grandpa in his stories.

Instead, the room was from another century. Heavy velvet curtains framed the windows. Before a double window, a Christmas tree stood. "Puny" was the word that came to mind. A sparse tree, hung with popcorn strings and very old and tired ornaments. No lights. No joy, except for wrapped gifts carefully and artistically arranged underneath. Most were for Mr. Sheridan, Julia noted.

Overstuffed, uncomfortable-looking furniture was placed, without grace, flanking an ornately carved table holding an artificial floral arrangement that might have overdecorated Queen Victoria's sideboard. A grand piano took up one corner of the large room, draped with a velvet tapestry and a display of what must have been some of Sheridan's trophies and awards. A settee actually reminded Julia of one her grandmother had had, horsehair stuffed and quite paralyzingly uncomfortable. Nobody had elected to sit on this one, either.

An older man in a tweed jacket detached himself from the piano on which he'd been leaning, and stepped forward. "I'm Forrest. Will Forrest. I live just across the field there." He gestured westward. "Walt was my oldest friend. I'd just come by, and the family was gathering in the foyer for lunch. We were waiting for Walt to join us."

A formal dinner seating could be expected in such a house, but lunch, in Julia's experience, was a casual come-and-go affair. "Was lunch served at the same time, or how did everyone know it was ready?"

"Oh, Walt insisted on regimentation. Cook was always ready to serve at one o'clock. She pushed a button at that time every afternoon. It rang a chime in every room of the house."

Phil Riley spoke up, his voice heavy with sarcasm. "So you just happened to come by exactly at lunch time?"

Will Forrest threw back his head and laughed. "You caught me. That's exactly what I did. Well, I did bring a Christmas present for Walt, but I really did time my visit so I might get a lunch invite. I'm not much of a cook myself, and I do enjoy company." He glanced around the room, his gaze resting longest on Mrs. Sheridan. "I guess I was terribly transparent. And this tragedy—well, it really isn't any of my business. So unless I'm needed here…"

"Hold it right there. Nobody leaves until the investigation is over. Sit."

He might be grumpy, but Lieutenant Riley had a commanding personality. Will Forrest sat.

Mrs. Sheridan moved into the conversation. "The meal schedules were what Walt wanted. Anyone late would not be seated and had to eat in the kitchen. I'm Walt's wife, Edna."

Julia had to lean in to hear her soft voice. Enormous doe-eyes dominated an otherwise plain face. Her dress was simply cut, with a white collar and cuffs. Simple and, surprisingly, not expensive. No jewelry adorned the outfit. And no engagement ring, Julia noted. Only a plain gold band on the left hand. And no tears.

"Edna's right. I'll vouch for that," a too-loud masculine voice stated. The young man moved in so quickly Julia had the impression of a St. Bernard puppy bounding up to play. "I was banished to the kitchen many a time. And got a royal ear-chewing after, too. Father's character was a benevolent old softy, but that was only on paper, believe me. The real Walt Sheridan was entirely different." He stuck out a slim hand. "I'm Sheridan, Junior. But I go by Wally. Father hated that." A conspiratorial smile lit his face.

Shaking hands with Wally Sheridan, Julia noted firm resolve and strength. She couldn't ignore the edge to his voice when he talked about his father's discipline. Physically warm and engaging, Wally made it clear his father was neither. Didn't like the old man. Possible suspect.

Again Phil Riley bulldozed his way into the discussion. "Edna? So she's not your mother?" Turning to Mrs. Sheridan, Phil turned on the Riley charm. "Too young, obviously. How long have you been married to the late Mr. Sheridan?"

The smile and charm weren't wasted on Julia. And the information was valuable.

"You're quite right, Lieutenant. Just five years now."

Wally put an arm around Edna's shoulder. "Edna was Father's nurse after he broke his ankle in a fall. He realized he couldn't do without her. And neither could the rest of us now." He beamed at his stepmother, who smiled back.

Julia made a mental note of the obvious affection the two shared. "Could everyone sit down again and let me introduce my squad. Then we want to view the, um, the late Mr. Sheridan. I'm afraid I'll have to ask you all to write down where you were and who you saw for about an hour before lunch up to the time the door was broken down. Then I'll ask you to come down to the station so we can question you individually. Freddie, please videotape everything in this room and then come film the crime scene."

"Crime scene? Are we under arrest?" The secretary looked from face to face. "But none of us would have anything to do with Walt's death. You can't think that."

Will Forrest winked at Mrs. Sheridan. It was a slight movement, but Julia didn't miss it. "Well, now," he said in a tone obviously meant to be jovial, "you will remember we were all getting ready to sit down to eat. In fact, as you made me confess, that's the reason I'm here. Can we get some sustenance if we go with you?"

Julia ground her teeth. The budget was tight for her squad, since they didn't have much major crime to deal with. No precedent for this. But no help for it. "We'll have some sandwiches brought in. But you'll all have to come as soon as you've written your statements, so we can secure and go over the scene. Sergeant Edgars, Officer Sykes, collect the papers, get them to me, and see that everyone leaves. One of you stay with them."

She glanced around at shocked faces. She smiled to lighten the atmosphere and spoke gently. "Put them in the conference room, make them comfortable, and call the diner to deliver sandwiches and soft drinks. Be sure an interrogation room is ready." Julia turned her palms up, spread her arms, and shrugged. "I'm sorry for this, but the sooner we conclude our investigation, the sooner we can release the site and the late Mr. Sheridan.

"This is Lieutenant Riley, Officer Sykes, Sergeant Edgars, and Freddie Majors. Please give them your cooperation and any answers they may require. Freddie, film every inch of both rooms. Lieutenant Riley, with me, please. And Sergeant Edgars, has the Robbery Division arrived to conduct the search?"

"Yes, ma'am."

"They'll be searching the premises after everyone's gone. They have the warrant? Good. Then everyone, write and then follow Officer Sykes, please."

Julia turned to Wally. "If you would just show us where…"

"Oh, of course. My father is in his study. This way, Chief." He led them a short way down a hall and pointed to a door hanging on its hinges, splintered wood strewn about the floor. "I had to break down the door to get to him. It was locked, you see. Excuse me. I'll leave you to it." And he escaped to join the others.

The squad entered Sheridan's study. Had Julia drawn a picture of what Walt Sheridan's special room would look like, she could have substituted it for the real thing and nobody would have noticed a difference. A true throwback man's den straight out of Hollywood. A fan of old films, Julia imagined Monte Woolley or Walter Pigeon at home there. The younger squad members were instantly tongue-tied and awe-struck. Built-in bookshelves lined the walls. Leather and mahogany.

Or not.

Julia was no expert, but the leather seemed faux and the furniture lacked the feel of old hardwood. Fireplace— but the lack of screen and a pair of hiking boots inside indicated it was non-functioning. Maybe never-functioning. The old-world imposing study was a replica. A stage set for America's Grandpa. She was tempted to pull books from the shelves, but she knew instinctively that, except for the Sheridan-written books on the nearest shelf, they were all just show. No well-thumbed leather-bound favorites there.

The body slumped across the typewriter on the desk, however, was quite real. So was the bullet hole in the right temple. Sheridan's right arm hung down as if he'd let go his weapon. But no gun lay on the floor. Or on the desk. Only an open copy of Sheridan's last book. And a pair of reading glasses. And the secretary's laptop.

There was no paper in the typewriter, Julia noted. That was odd.

"Look for the gun. Or a casing. And the bullet, since it passed through the skull. It should be somewhere in the bookshelf—maybe inside a book. And dust for prints, though they'll show everyone in the family and on staff have been here. Bag his hands, so we can test for gunshot residue."

Though if they found residue, she didn't know what they would make of it without a weapon.

She stepped back, surveying the entire room. "Check the windows carefully. See if there's any way anyone could have gotten in or out with them locked. Make sure the fireplace isn't actually an entry point. Everyone examine the bookcases for hidden entries." But as she spoke, she knew in her gut she stood in what had been the quintessential locked room.

Suicide. No note. No apparent motive. And no gun.

Riley spoke up. "May I, Chief? Before you guys from Robbery leave, search all the premises. Any one of these people might have had time to ditch a weapon, and they know this house. How they'd do it without someone knowing it—that's for our squad to find out. My gut tells me they'd be watching each other, and if anyone went somewhere else in the house, someone would see it, so pay closest attention to this room and the living room. You're looking for a weapon, but anything else might shed some light on this mess."

He turned to Julia and gestured to the door. "Chief, shall we let the guys work?"

She looked around the room one more time, the light-canceling dark wood, the dusty volumes, the shoddiness of the deception. She stopped in the door of the living room and scanned the oppressively heavy drapes, the unwelcoming furnishings, the cheap tree, and the gaudy presents, like tributes paid to the emperor. What a way to celebrate Christmas.

Guilt sagged her shoulders. She'd worked so hard to establish competence. But now, with the whole country looking on, she had no method to make it a murder and no weapon to prove suicide.

Put it out of your mind, like you told everyone to do. She was going to stay home for a half hour, grab a bite, and refrigerate some dough for Christmas cookies so they'd be ready to bake later tonight. Meyer's Market was on the next corner.

She popped into the store and bought a bag of walnuts and cream cheese. "Nutcracker Nibbles. Perfect choice to make. Nutcracker for Christmas, and cracking nuts of alibis and meagre evidence to solve the Great Grandpa Demise. Nothing like a good metaphor to muddy the investigation even more."

Jamming her grocery bag into her ever-present tote, she turned the corner onto Destin Avenue and her house. The only still undecorated house in her block. She really must do something about that. A nice display would show her neighbors a spirit of cooperation, and when she took them her homemade pastries, she'd bank even more good will. The neighbors seemed to be nice enough, but she'd been busy moving in and settling into the new job, so she didn't know any of them really well. No time for coffee and gossip over the back fence. Yet. She had to fix that, because her work by itself wouldn't give her much of a life. And she'd moved here to make one.

So far the only near-conversation she'd had in the neighborhood was exchanging waves with a little girl three houses down. The girl was in her front yard frequently, always wearing a tutu and dancing about. "Before I take cookies there, I must find and include my precious Tom Tierney ballerina paper dolls. Nutcracker Nibbles and Nutcracker dancers. It's Sugar Plum Fairy season, and I think the dolls would have a good new home."

Silly the things one kept, but this time hanging on to a bit of the past might net her a new friend for the future, even if she wasn't much older than five or six. And it might add a grateful mother, delighted if her child spent hours designing and cutting out costumes for the dolls, as Julia had when she was that age and had her own tutu. She'd even appeared in a production of *The Nutcracker*, long ago. Mentally, she did a pirouette.

"Hey, Chief. Chief Dunnigan. Wait up."

The voice and running feet brought her thoughts abruptly back to police business. Lieutenant Phil Riley was chugging after her. That tingle started in her knees again, and she waited for him. Thank goodness she hadn't actually tried a dance step. A woman over forty twirling around suddenly would look demented. And could break something.

"Glad I caught up with you. Listen, Chief, this case is really bothering me. Mind if I walk with you and go over the interrogation information? I know you want us to clear our minds, but I can't. Maybe if we go over it once more…"

"Sure, Lieutenant. My head won't let go of it either. C'mon."

They walked together silently for a few steps. Julia tried to believe she was letting Phil catch his breath, but in truth, her own wasn't so steady anymore. And she had to concentrate on her tingling knees.

She turned in to her house, and Riley stopped cold. "Oh, Chief. You probably have things planned to do. I can…"

"Come right on in, Lieutenant Riley. I'm going to mix some cookie dough, but I can talk and do that at the same time. No problem. In fact, I'll put you to work, if you don't mind. And feed you, since everyone else is eating at the station. I just had to get a change of scenery."

She led him to the kitchen, where he perched on a stool at the island.

"If you're sure. Okay, then. I keep thinking we're missing something. And those alibis—too neat. Too ready."

Julia set the walnuts and cream cheese on the counter and paused before reaching for the flour canister. "I know exactly what you mean. Rehearsed. In fact, the whole scene seemed practiced. Of course, they had time to discuss their stories while they waited for us to arrive." She shook her head. "We'll never know for sure what anyone really did or said."

She put the bag of walnuts and two bowls in front of Riley. Then she lifted down from a display ledge her family treasure—the nutcracker her mother had given her in honor of her debut as a mouse in the beloved ballet. She set it in front of Riley along with a pick.

He blinked at it. "You do know you can buy these

things already shelled."

"But then you lose the satisfaction of involvement. And it's therapeutic."

She raised her eyebrows and smiled at him. "We know there were sixteen minutes between the lunch bell and our arrival. Not much time there. But how long had he been dead before that bell?" She put a pan on the stove and lit the burner. She didn't turn back until she heard the satisfying crack of a nutshell opening.

"Time of death is vague, too, so how much time did they actually have before they called us?" Phil Riley's eyes almost glistened. "I mean, most civilians have no clue that time of death can't be narrowed like it is on television, but they do know there's wiggle room. If they want to hide something." Crack.

Julia paused at the refrigerator and turned back to him. "Like the gun. Damn that gun. That locked door. And damn that Wally for breaking it down. Nothing to examine now."

"Right, Chief." Crack.

Julia reached into the fridge and pulled out butter and a container holding her homemade tomato soup. Satisfying and tangy. She'd been famous for this soup in her last town. One elderly man had even proposed to her after eating it. Maybe it would loosen the shell around this lieutenant. She poured the soup into a saucepan and slid it onto the heat, forcing her voice to be casual.

"Um... would you just call me Julia? While we're in my kitchen, at least? That would make this speculation less formal. So we won't have to write reports."

"Oh. Well, I could try. For a cup of real coffee. And I'm..."

"Phil. I know." She stuck out her hand and shook his,

smiling. Miraculously, Phil smiled back.

Heat swam up her neck and onto her cheeks. She was holding his hand. A little too long. She let go abruptly and mumbled, "Coffee." Her legs somehow took her across the floor to the coffeemaker, and she fumbled a pod into the slot. "Black, I presume?"

"How did you… Oh. Yeah, black is fine."

Black was the perpetual flavor du jour at the station. There was a rotation list on the station bulletin board showing who was in charge of bringing in sugar and creamer. The list was fly-specked and yellowing. Several of the people listed no longer worked there. Nobody had brought any condiments since she'd been there.

Keep moving. She poured two mugs of steaming coffee and set them on the island. She opened a cabinet and got out a bowl and a pastry cutter, trying to be as quiet as she could. "So. Shall we start with the first interview? That was…"

"The cook. Okay, she was working on lunch. Had to be ready by one or else. Or else what, she didn't make clear, but she didn't like the old guy and his schedules."

"Or his budgets," Julia added, working her pastry cutter on the butter and cream cheese and flour. The pressure and rocking motion soothed her, but she could imagine Sheridan's cook gouging at the mixture aggressively, muttering about her tightwad boss. "Still, she could quit. A cook could probably get a job anywhere. No reason to kill an employer. Unless he were making indecent advances, but she outweighed him and was armed with frying pans and rolling pins."

Phil snorted, and his coffee splashed. She laughed, too, and handed him a paper towel.

"And then Mrs. Sheridan came in to set up menus for

17

the next week." Julia leaned against the island and looked into space. "That seems like the worst possible timing, since Grandpa insisted on his one o'clock deadline."

"Right. Doesn't ring true. Wonder if the widow turned to a little blackmail to force that alibi."

"So we agree. Two suspicious alibis. And maybe both women resented his stranglehold on money. The wife seemed to have no say in what was spent and what happened when. She didn't sound resentful, but that sort of thing festers over time. Who was next?"

"The secretary. She was certainly tense. I'd say she was pissed off about something." Crack.

"I agree with that, too." Julia slapped the dough onto the counter, shaped it into a rectangle, wrapped it in plastic, and stuck it into the refrigerator. The activity felt good, and Phil watched her every move. His attention felt very good.

She took out cheese and more butter, sliced homemade bread into thick slabs, grilled some cheese sandwiches, and plated them with bowls of her tomato soup. When she put it down in front of him, a grin spread across his face. "That really smells good. Sure beats the diner. Thanks, Chie…I mean, Julia."

She settled in beside him with her own steaming plate of comfort food.

"The secretary. When Sykes and I asked her how Mr. Sheridan and his valet got along, she hesitated for a bit too long, didn't you think? Before she admitted Mr. Sheridan didn't treat him with any respect. Being ignored and overlooked and taken for granted—that sort of thing can weigh a person down. Believe me, I know."

Phil shot a look at her, but ignored her personal remark and pressed on. "She did try to pin a motive for killing the old gent on him, while being very careful not to push it, seems like. And Sheridan wasn't that kind to her, either. The valet told me and Edgars she confessed the old guy was losing it. That she had to clean up a lot of his work and she re-wrote about half of it."

"Hmmm. Interesting. Was he going to give her credit?"

"The valet thought no, that she did it out of concern for his reputation. If the public found out the old boy couldn't write anymore, she'd be out of a prestigious job, and her reference would lose credibility."

"Hmmm. If Sheridan were unable to function, not only her reputation would suffer. The public would shy away from a surrogate problem-solving Grandpa with lots of problems of his own. Might dry up the franchise."

Julia got up, gathered a legal pad and pen, and sat back down. She listed those who had been present in the house. Labeling one column ALIBI and another MOTIVE, she turned to look at Phil.

He picked up his plate so he could turn to face her. Their knees touched. Neither shifted.

"Secretary alibis valet; valet alibis secretary. He was treated badly over a long period. She was doing work she'd never get credit for. Two suspects, each with a motive."

Then her pad dropped to her lap and her chin to her chest. "But the room was locked."

"Yes," said Phil. "But. We have no weapon. Somebody is guilty. Maybe Sheridan offed himself, but maybe...not."

She stiffened as if re-inflating herself. "Of course. The door was broken, but we only have their word about when it happened."

"Or why."

Julia rose and began to pace. "Right. So anyone could be a murderer. Including Sheridan himself, of course. Is there any way to tell when wood was splintered?"

"Not that I know of."

"Then we still have to find the weapon. I sealed off the study and the living room—were you ever anywhere more uncomfortable in your life?—but we'd better re-interview everyone with an eye to motives. Ready to go back? They'll be finished with lunch at the station by now."

****

"Sorry to trouble you further, Mrs. Sheridan," Julia apologized to the widow. "We know this day has been horrible. But we have to clear up some routine loose ends before the coroner can release your husband. Won't you sit?"

The birdlike woman dropped to a seat in the interrogation room obediently. Like a trained animal, Julia thought. "You said you were with the cook. Were you helping with lunch preparation?"

"Oh, no. I would never interfere with Cook's work. She wouldn't like it."

"But it was your kitchen," Phil said gruffly. "Just how long were you there before the lunch was ready?"

"I think it…um…must have been about an hour."

"An hour?" Phil's voice was even harsher. "To set a weekly menu? How could that take so long?"

Mrs. Sheridan seemed to shrink. "Um…well…we had to inventory any weekly leftovers. Then we had to price every ingredient out so we conformed to budget. Neither of us is very good with math, I'm afraid. Then I helped her put away the clean breakfast dishes. I don't know…" She clenched her hands.

"Still, an hour?"

"Mrs. Sheridan," Julia said gently. Suddenly they were playing good cop/ bad cop. "It was nice of you to help with the dishes. I know this is difficult, but how well did you know the cook? And what sort of relationship did she have with Mr. Sheridan?"

"Oh, relationship? Well, she'd been there for years. Before I came, in fact. They didn't seem to like each other much. She hated the low budget she had to work with. And I know she disliked being on a strict timetable. She told me that once she missed the six o'clock call to dinner, and Sheridan said he'd fire her and destroy any chance she'd work anywhere in the county. Well, he said 'state,' but I think he exaggerated his sphere of influence." At this, she almost smiled, but quickly lowered her head.

Phil burst out, "So why did she stay? He couldn't have been serious."

"Oh, I think you'll find Walt Sheridan did not threaten what he didn't intend to carry out. But…he was a great man. We were privileged to be in his circle. Are you through with me? I'm feeling a bit lightheaded, and I want this to be over." Without waiting for a response, she rose and tottered from the room.

"There's one browbeaten woman," Phil observed, shaking his shaggy head.

"Maybe she was always that way, and marriage to Sheridan lent her needed security. We'll get Freddie to dig into her background to see what sort of past she came from."

"Yeah. I can see whatever she came from could have made this gig look almost good. How 'bout that 'great man' comment! Like a robot. But what would he get out of the marriage?"

"Someone new to dominate?"

Phil shook his head again and went to get the cook.

Stereotypically, she was what Julia thought of as beefy. Squinty-eyed suspicious, too. She denied resenting the financial and time constraints.

"So Mrs. Sheridan says she was with you for an hour before you rang the lunch bell. Can you confirm that?"

Cook's eyes widened and briefly darted to the left. "She said that, did she? She was there all right. Interfering in my planning. But I shooed her away. I had to have lunch ready by one. Can't have distractions in my kitchen."

"Know where she went when she left you?"

"Don't know. Don't care." Cook rose, indicating that whether or not their questions were done, she was. Phil half rose to detain her, but Julia shook her head at him, thanked her, and said good night.

"I coulda stopped her, you know."

"Oh, I'm sure. But I don't think she knows anything, really. And I'm not so very sure Mrs. Sheridan's lie is serious. I want to talk to the secretary."

Phil ushered the secretary, Miss Boynton, into the interrogation room. Once she was seated, he barked suddenly, "Is it true you ghost wrote a good deal of Sheridan's work?"

Her hands flew to her cheeks. "Where did you hear...?" Then, recovering her composure she said, "That's just common practice. A bit of editing and proofing along the way. He was showing his age a bit, but he was a great man and a great writer. Besides, he never watched the shows or read the books. He never knew. Is that all?"

"Just one more question, please. We know you're busy. But have you plans for the future? New home? New job?"

Miss Boynton's eyes went steely, and her lips formed a tight smile. "Mrs. Sheridan invited me to stay on. Indefinitely." She leaned forward conspiratorially and actually whispered, "She believes her husband may have held back some writing over the years. We need a full inventory of his papers, which may take…quite a while. Excuse me." She rose and strode out of the room.

Phil walked a few steps after her before turning. "Don't know about you, but I'm getting pretty suspicious about how many times that 'great man' story comes up."

Julia slapped her hands on the table. "You're right. It's a pattern. Nobody seems to have really liked him, but they all say he was a 'great man.' And how about that possible unpublished work? And the secretary staying on indefinitely?"

A knock on the door alerted them Edgars had returned.

"You'd better have some good news," Riley warned.

Edgars' mouth twitched. "I sure have, well, something. I checked with Sheridan's attorney, like you said, Chief. Apparently when the television deal came up years ago, Sheridan was strapped for money. Dirt poor. So he took a single payment for the TV rights and a small writer's fee for story ideas the network accepted. He didn't actually write many episodes. In the credits, other writers were always listed, and Sheridan got a 'created by' credit. The network owned the rights and residuals. And merchandising, so Sheridan didn't even get full royalties for the books."

"Which he didn't write either," Riley said.

"The attorney said he couldn't get Sheridan to draw up a will. He pressed Sheridan to make one, but the old man was too tight to pay for it."

"Who knew about the financials? Was the family aware?"

"I knew that would be important, Chief. The attorney said Wally Sheridan certainly knew. He'd come to the office to discuss finances a few months ago."

"So," Julia said, "nobody benefits from the death?"

A broad this-could-mean-a-promotion grin split Edgars' face. "Well. About that. The Robbery guys couldn't find a weapon. But they did find this." With a flourish, he produced a document. "It's an insurance policy. Found it in the son's desk."

Riley snatched the papers from Edgars' hand. One glance and he shouted, "Here's a motive, Chief. Three months ago, an insurance policy was taken out on the old geezer. Five million dollars. That's a hunk of cash to kill for." Riley stopped waving the papers and slowly lowered his hand and his voice. "But…"

"Locked room," said Julia. "And too many witnesses, as you already said."

Edgars rocked heel to toe. "Look at the rest of the papers, Riley. I think you'll find…"

Phil Riley ripped through the papers. "We got 'em. Look, Chief."

Julia took the last two sheets. A schedule of premium payments listed who would pay for which month. While the valet and maid shared a payment, each of the others was responsible for making a full month's payment. The final sheet was a signed agreement by all. There had been a reason Wally visited the attorney, something the lawyer hadn't mentioned—attorney/living client privilege.

"Conspiracy, Chief. They've been conspiring for months. But was it murder or suicide?"

Riley snapped his fingers. "The only person without any real alibi is that neighbor, Forrest. He's not part of the insurance thing. So what was he doing there? From what we've heard, with the strict kitchen budget, lunch wouldn't have been anything special enough to want to share. And old friend or not, our old skinflint wouldn't have overlooked a blatant attempt to glom onto his food."

"You're right, Lieutenant. Let's talk to Mr. Forrest."

Will Forrest came into the interrogation room brushing breadcrumbs off his shirt. "I said I wanted lunch, true, but I didn't expect the city would be buying it for me. Thank you." Julia was seated behind the table, and Riley ignored Forrest's outstretched hand.

"Have a seat, Forrest. Now, we've been hearing a lot about how Walt Sheridan squeezed every nickel. So why would he allow drop-ins at his table?"

Forrest stopped short of sitting down, straightened, and hesitated for a little too long. "Well, first, I was a guest of his wife. But you're right about Sheridan. He was a lifelong friend, but he wasn't generous. Still…" A smile lit Forrest's face. "I brought him a Christmas present. The old miser couldn't turn me away without worrying I'd take that gift away with me." Forrest sat down and spread his hands out on the table expansively. "Sort of presented him with a financial dilemma, don't you see? It amused me to think he'd have to invite me to break bread because he wouldn't know if the present was worth more or less than the lunch."

He leaned back in his chair, clearly pleased with himself. "Of course, just about anything would be. Worth more, I mean. I just liked to mess with his mind. What are friends for?"

****

After Forrest left, Julia asked to be alone to think. There was something—if she could just figure out what. Pacing usually helped. Up and down the narrow hallway she went, seeing nothing, turned inward.

Great man.

Tarnished reputation.

Practiced alibis that seemed to crumble.

The secretary staying on salary to search for "unpublished (read unsold) works."

The lack of warmth in the household.

So many people who stayed when leaving would serve them better.

The looks that passed between Edna and Will Forrest.

The impossibility of the missing weapon and the locked room.

The insurance policy Sheridan had never seen and everyone invested in.

Forrest's last remark. *What are friends for?*

That was it!

But she needed proof. She needed two things.

"Freddie! Bring me the video. Lieutenant, help me look, please."

"What are we looking for?" Riley asked, chugging into the murder room in her wake.

"The rooms. Imagine you're one of the guys from Robbery searching for the gun. What would you investigate most closely? Watch."

The study flashed on the screen. Freddie slowly panned every inch, starting with ground level and moving up the bookcases. He spent time zooming in on objects on the desk.

"See? His last book. Open. Miss Boynton said he never looked at them. And no paper in the typewriter. He never wrote his two new pages. Didn't even try. He must have known he…"

"He couldn't do it anymore." Riley's eyes widened. "Or ever could. Right. Good motive for a suicide, if we had a gun. But I still don't know what we're looking for."

"That's all right, Phil. It's the other room I want you to concentrate on."

The picture jumped, became a sweep of the horribly misnamed living room. Floor level. Then up a degree and the pan around the room. Slowly, Freddie revealed the dreadful furniture, the piano and awards, the sad tree. Up along the drapes. Around the ceiling.

"Okay. Imagine you're Robbery. Where do you look?" This time her question included Edgars and Sykes, who had drifted over and peered at the screen.

"Well, I assume I'm looking for the gun, right? So I'd pat down the furniture, check the bottoms and the backs for openings to stuff something in. Behind the drapes. Under the tapestries. In that awful floral sprawl— you could hide almost anything in that monstrosity."

"And…"

"Piano. You'd have to remove all those prizes to get inside the piano, but that's a huge hiding place."

"Right. But as you say, everything would have to be moved and replaced."

"And that takes time. Makes a commotion. Someone would have seen or heard."

"You've got it. That's a crack in the nut."

"What nut?" Phil's raised eyebrows wrinkled his

forehead.

"The nut of the case. Oh, never mind. I'm not crazy. But it comes down to that. Somebody would have seen or heard. You said that before, Lieutenant Riley."

"Look, I'm usually pretty good at this, but you lost me. What are you talking about? And what are we looking for in this video? What do you know that I can't see? Are you thinking secret drawers in the furniture?"

"No. Look again. Run the video back to the start of the living room. Because that's where the gun is."

Phil shook his head. "I don't see it."

"That's just the point. You don't see it, because it's in plain sight. Wait. Let's think about motive. You said failing ability was a motive for suicide, right?"

Julia got up and began pacing again. Sergeant Edgars, Officer Sykes, and Freddie watched her and cast sidelong confused glances at each other.

She stopped and turned to her audience. "If Edna had a motive, what would it be?"

"She hated the old man," Freddie said.

"Resentment. All that money and she lived in a terrible house and ate cheap food." This from Sergeant Edgars.

"Well, right," Julia said. "Those are motives. But why didn't she just leave?"

"I get it," Sykes said. "The money was there, and she'd lose all claim to it. After all she'd invested. Time, humiliation, lovelessness. She'd want her share. She'd earned it."

"But that was everyone's motive. The secretary hated doing the creative work with no reward. But with Sheridan gone, she could keep on doing the work but with the wife paying proper dividends."

"Right. And the servants could be paid decently. There would be money for living luxuriously. As long as Sheridan's reputation was gold."

"And the work kept coming."

Phil tilted his head. "But. There wasn't any money."

"No real reputation. No royalties from book sales. Nothing from television. No money." Julia wiped a sheen of perspiration from her forehead. "Wally found that out. And suddenly there was a whopping insurance policy. They were all in it together. Like Forrest said, 'What are friends for?' "

"Soooo." Phil sat down and stared at his shoes, working it out aloud. "They discovered a suicide. At least one of them realized the consequences of that. Insurance policies have suicide clauses, and theirs could be worthless. They couldn't hide the death. But they could make it a mystery. What you might call…" He looked up and wagged his forefinger at Julia. "What you might call an uncrackable nut. All they had to do was figure out mutual alibis for everyone, lock the door and break it down—and hide the gun."

All eyes went to the Chief.

"They didn't have much time. So they hid the gun in plain sight. In a place nobody would search, until there was time to dispose of it properly. Let's go back to the house and see if I'm right."

****

The living room showed signs of searching. The awards were on the floor, the velvet throw tossed over the piano bench. The floral arrangement would never be the same. All furniture had been shifted, some turned upside down and not righted again. Drapes were bunched in knots that lifted them off the floor.

The squad looked around, but light did not dawn in their eyes.

"I'm right. One thing hasn't changed a bit. Even the guys from Robbery steered clear. Because it's Christmas."

All eyes zeroed in on the brightly wrapped boxes under the sorry tree. Not one had been touched.

"Do not open until…" Phil swooped down, located the gift from Will Forrest, and lifted it high. "Has weight. This is it." He tore at the wrappings, lifted the box lid, and whooped.

"We got 'em, Chief. They're all guilty. The whole kit and kaboodle."

"Wait," Freddie said. "Guilty of what? The old guy committed suicide, after all."

Phil Riley grimaced and threw up his arms. "Conspiracy? Obstruction of justice? Whatever we charge them with, we'll never get finished with the damned paperwork before New Year's."

Elation evaporated from the room.

Julia gazed into each face.

Her squad. The family she'd be baking Nutcracker Nibbles for tonight.

"Those people have all been so very unhappy. And now they can't count on new income. New jobs will be compromised, insurance won't pay, and the house will be difficult to sell with the connection to a suicide of such national interest. They're all guilty, yes, but their pasts have been nothing but punishment, and their futures may be grim."

She could see the team was with her. But rules were rules.

Phil Riley nodded. "I happen to know the D.A. loves

Christmas. And he owes me some favors. After all, he's my brother-in-law. I'll bet I can talk him into just accepting this one as suicide and let it—and them—go. Just as long…" He moved to Julia's side. "Just as long as there are cookies tomorrow." He bent close to whisper in her ear. "I'd be happy to come help you finish them. And maybe take you to dinner?"

"I'd be delighted, Lieutenant Riley. After all…" Her knees tingled, and something secret passed between them. Something that wouldn't stay secret for long. "Anything can happen at Christmas."

Death by Gingerbread Drops

by

Jo A. Hiestand

Christmas Cookies Series

Dedication

To M-H, the first baker I knew.

Chapter One

"From the look of the parking lot there's a large crowd here this evening," Johnny Murray noted. "The Bake-Up should make a lot of money, Rona."

"Well, let's hope so. That is the plan," Rona said as her ex, his arms loaded with boxes of Christmas cookies, stomped the snow from his boots just outside the café entrance.

Once inside, he glanced around the main room and marveled, "Wow, look at this place."

Rona had to admit the transformation from a normal restaurant into a wintry festival was impressive. Paper snowflakes and glass icicles hung from the ceiling. The usual artwork had been removed from the walls, and had been replaced by wreaths, leaving space for various other holiday décor. Christmas songs played, and the aromas of hot chocolate and warm spices floated on the air.

"Mmm, cookie aromas." Johnny took a deep breath. "Smells like your place. Very nice."

"Flattery will get you nowhere. You already had a cookie on the way over here." Rona owned the Linn House bakery. She shifted the silvery platters she carried under her arm as the recorded music floating from the café's music system changed to "I'll Be Home for Christmas." Rona looked around the room, suspecting someone of reading her thoughts and broadcasting the apropos song. But she saw no one standing by the CD player beside the cash register. Maybe Santa really did know what people wanted.

Even though she and Johnny had been divorced for a year, she admitted the hasty decision had been a mistake. Since their chance meeting several months ago, it became more apparent each time they spent time together it was a decision she wished she could reverse. Was she too old to tell Santa that what she really wanted for Christmas was a reconciliation?

The sound of Johnny's voice pulled her out of her contemplation. "…I should buy a box of cookies for myself and eat them in the car."

"I thought you had supper before you picked me up," she turned and said.

"I did. But that was almost an hour ago. Besides, I left room for dessert. I'm determined to get something here. I'm starving. That one measly cookie you gave me was hardly enough to classify it as dessert. A handful would've been better."

"Thanks for the compliment, but you're always saying you're trying to lose ten pounds. Not that you need to." Shifting her gaze to her ex-husband's tall figure, she admired his physique. She mutely admitted, although his waist had thickened somewhat over time, he was still trim enough to be considered in good shape. A touch of gray in his brown hair gave him that distinguished look women seldom acquire as they grayed. Never mind that he was fifty-seven, he looked in better shape than most men she knew.

"That cookie—that *one* little cookie—was for the ride here, Rona. In addition to my postponed dessert, I'll need another one for the ride back to your house. I thought you could get me some samples."

"Not a chance." She shook her head and gave him her don't play me look, but said, "Thanks for picking me up, by the way."

"That's okay. This morning's horoscope said I needed to heed today's reading."

"And what did it say, or shouldn't I ask?"

"Share the evening with a friend." His right eyebrow rose.

She ran her hand across her mouth, hiding her smile, and nodded toward the row of tables to their right. "Look at all the choices you have. I hope you've brought enough money."

"Probably not," he said.

"This is a fundraiser. There aren't any freebies. Gol, I bet everyone in Klim is here."

Klim, Missouri—perched on the western bluff of the Mississippi River—probably wasn't much different from other small Midwestern towns, with its grain and feed store, specialty shops, and white clapboard churches. And though she wasn't seeing life through rose-tinted glasses, it at least seemed golden-hued to Rona. Family, Mark Twain's river, and pirate lore were mixed and embodied in the town's five and a half square miles. That acreage included the river, she mentally appended, with imagines of its sandbars and tree-choked cliffs shimmering in her mind's eye.

"So many wonderful aromas." She inhaled, smiling and half-shutting her eyes.

Johnny sniffed the air in several directions. "Other than the cookies, I don't smell anything so great. It's just the usual evergreens and cold air. Is the door shut?"

Rona sighed heavily and took a deep breath. "Don't get overly romantic. It's only the Yuletide."

"It's just the sort of thing that also brings on my allergies."

"Poor baby."

"Can I help it if I'm sensitive?" He patted her ski cap. "That color blue suits you, Ronnie. Compliments your red hair."

"This thing?" His comment made her cheeks burn or maybe it was from coming inside. "I'm surprised it's retained its color." She stuffed the cap into her slacks pocket and tried to sound irritated, but only succeeded in laughing. "Truth be told, my grandparents gave it to me, and I won't say how many years ago that was."

"Well, you've taken good care of it. Looks new. So does the café," he added, taking in the bar area and the dozens of tables. "Great space."

"You didn't know the café when it was an art gallery. Chad's worked extremely hard and put in long hours making it a first-class establishment. There used to be a wall of glass blocks facing the street, there. He tore them out and put in strips of corrugated iron and wood, and these huge windows. Gives it the arts-and-crafts atmosphere and compliments the artwork usually hanging on the walls. And the original sign over the doorway was repainted into the current river scene."

"And he named this place Dante's Café after your bakery, right?"

"In a way. It's actually a nod to the Devil's Bar brownies I created. The Devil's Bar—the sandy spit of land where my great grandparents built their first residence on the river—and the Devil popping up on Chad's interior walls through the illustrations from Dante's *Inferno*."

"You should be proud, Rona. Not many people are

so honored. He must think a lot of you. As do others."

This time when heat flooded her cheeks, she knew his compliment was the reason She tried to think of a flippant reply, something in the vein of their usual tit-for-tat, pseudo verbal sparring. She was spared the embarrassment of not being able to come up with a retort when someone announced over the PA system that the auction would begin in fifteen minutes.

She grabbed his hand and said, "Come on. I've got to get these cookies checked-in and onto some platters." Rona threaded her way through the crowd, toward the kitchen, Johnny in tow.

The restaurant's kitchen resembled what she always imagined Santa's workshop could be like if the jolly old man distributed cookies instead of toys. Boxes and plates of baked goods blanketed every flat space. The swinging door constantly moved as people brought in their donations and volunteers carried filled trays out to the main room.

Johnny drew in a lungful of the warm air, apparently oblivious to the hubbub of chatter and music. "Ah. Baked goods. This is heaven."

Rona tilted her head back, staring at the ceiling and sighing before turning toward a large metal worktable that was all but smothered with donated baked items.

"Rona!" Debbie Weingarten grabbed the trays from Rona and kissed her cheek. Middle-aged and with a few streaks of gray in her otherwise brunette hair, the woman seemed unruffled about finding a place among the other boxes of cookies surrounding her. It looked as if it would take an army of volunteers to get all the baked goods on to the auction tables. But since the cookies were set out in groups as they sold, everything didn't have to be unpacked and on view at the same time. Besides, Debbie had worked the auction for years—a few more dozen donations wouldn't throw her. As she was fond of saying, "I enjoy thinking I'm like yeast: I rise to the occasion."

Debbie glanced at the kitchen wall clock and spoke above the chatter in the room. "Glad you got here. I hear the weather's going to get bad later." She set the trays on the only clear space and stepped aside as Johnny stacked the cookie boxes beside them. "Hi, Johnny. I see Rona roped you into helping."

"If she needed muscles, I'm the obvious choice." He winced as Rona elbowed him in his ribs.

"You doing anything special for Christmas, Rona? I suppose your events center is booked solid with seasonal dinners and such."

"Fairly solid, yes. I think I'm hosting lunches nearly every day for two solid weeks, including the week between Christmas and New Year's."

"Well, 'tis the season, as they say." Debbie undid the string around the top carton and draped it across the top of an empty container. "Wish I could bake as well as you and your staff do, but I never had the talent. My mom always said I was better at thinking than of doing."

"The world needs thinkers as well as doers."

"True, but I'd like to do occasionally." She eyed Johnny, who stood beside Rona, his right arm draped around her shoulders. "You have any Christmas plans, Johnny?"

"A few, but I'm not sure if one of them will come to fruition."

"Is your family flying in from somewhere? Of course, it depends on the weather."

"No, but it all depends on whether or not a family member once removed likes my idea."

Debbie pushed up the sleeves of her sweater and frowned. "Sounds cryptic, but it's nothing to do with me."

"What about you? You cooking dinner for your neighbor like you did last year?"

"I don't know. I put the feelers out a week ago, but he said he might be out of town. He didn't know yet. I told him I always cook a whole turkey, and he can come over Christmas afternoon if he's in town."

"That's nice."

"I thought so, but he just made noncommittal noises and said he didn't know and that I shouldn't count on him, but he'd drop in for an eggnog even if he couldn't come for dinner. I don't know." Debbie exhaled loudly, as though she was already tired. "I didn't think dinner would be such a huge decision. I mean, you eat, don't you? What difference does it make if you eat a frozen meal at home or trot next door to a homemade affair?"

Rona shrugged and Johnny's arm dropped from her shoulders. "There's no telling, Debbie. People have priorities different from ours. Maybe he's got back-up plans. Anyway, if he was over last year and enjoyed it, you might see him again."

"I hope so. The man's losing weight, if you ask me."

Rona glanced at Johnny, unsure of how to reply. Well…" She forced a brightness into her voice she didn't feel. "Is this all I need to do?"

"That's it."

"All this looks overwhelming. Are you sure you don't need help? I can stay if—"

"I've got coworkers, thanks. Chad will be back any

minute to grab some more trays and take them into the main room, and Angela's in and out of here constantly. We'll get everything out in time."

"If you say so." Rona eyed the dozens of other cookies being arranged on trays and platters.

Debbie opened the top box and smiled. "Lovely! Are these your famous Gingerbread Drops?"

"Don't know about famous, but they're Gingerbread Drops."

"I'll have to stop by your bakery and get some when I shed a few pounds. I adore anything gingerbread." She picked one up. "Incredible, spicy aroma. Nicely decorated too," she added, admiring the stars, evergreens and bells piped on with icing. "The bidding should be lively on these. I'd bid myself, but…" Her hand plopped onto her stomach and she winced. "Unfortunately, cookies are my secret vice. Just look through my old wardrobe of size ten clothes if you need proof. Oh well…" She began placing the cookies on a metal platter.

"I brought five dozen of those. They're in the top two boxes. The other box holds four dozen sugar cookies."

"Expertly decorated, if I know you. Your bakery deserves its fine reputation."

"My bakers had nothing to do with these, I'll have you know. I made them, as the event rules stipulate."

"Well, I'm sure they'll go as fast as kids opening presents on Christmas. Thanks."

The overhead lights in the main room dimmed momentarily, then sprang back to life as Glenn Somers—a detective in the Klim, Missouri police department—spoke into the microphone. Tall and dark haired, Glenn always said his life was filled with crime and cookies, but there was never a hesitation over which he liked the most. The annual Bake-Up a Cookie Storm fundraiser was not only his brainchild but also his passion. Where else can you get a warm glow in your heart from helping children and a warm glow in your stomach from eating wonderful cookies? Probably many places, but he had no desire to find out. Right now, he was happy to be surrounded by cookies and warm-hearted people, most of whom he called his friends. He cleared his throat as he stood at the mike, waiting for the room to quiet before he greeted everyone.

"He's about to start the auction, Rona," Johnny whispered into her ear, his lips unnecessarily close.

"And he always says the same things." Rona nodded toward the wall displaying several dozen wreaths in assorted sizes, styles, and evergreens. "I'm impressed with the variety of wreaths people donated this year. They should also bring in a substantial amount for the auction." Rona sipped her hot cider and stared at a holly-and-ivy twined wreath on the wall. "That's really nice. I may buy it at the auction or find out who donated it if I can't get it."

"You can do that, later. Glenn's handing your platter of Gingerbread Drops to Angela. Look." Johnny nudged her and nodded toward the tables of cookies that paralleled the café's west wall.

Rona turned toward the auction area as a thirty-year-old woman, dressed in a red sweater and winter-white skirt, set her drink on the table, and picked up a red-and-white iced cookie. Glenn's voice came over the café's loudspeakers in an easy way that left the listener no doubt the man had been introducing the charity for years.

"Thank you for coming this Friday evening,

especially in spite of the wintry weather." He paused as people glanced outside at the falling snow. "Regardless of what you think, I had nothing to do with the appropriate timing. Although the snowstorm does put me in the mood for a storm of cookies."

Someone called out that he hoped everyone was welcome to camp out in the café and munch the auction donations if the storm got too bad.

"Anyway, I hope the wintry weather adds the appropriate mood to our event and that it helps put you in the right spirit to purchase your favorite cookies, no matter the price…" He paused as several people laughed or applauded. "Well, I'll be happy. And of course, thanks to everyone who baked up a storm for this year's charity event. The lucky bidders on these cookies will no doubt be doubly glad of their wins, if I'm to believe the local lore about spoon-shaped kernels in the persimmons I recently bought. And, if correct," he added, speaking slowly and looking around the group, "I hope the hardware store will run a sale on snow shovels."

When the laughter subsided, Glenn continued. "I also hope your wallets will be as open as your hearts have been previously for this event. Every penny raised this evening benefits Klim, Missouri's Children First Charitable Foundation. The kids get your help, and you get incredibly superb cookies baked by our area's finest bakers." He glanced at Angela, who looked wistfully at the cookie, as if she couldn't wait another moment to take a bite. "Now, my co-chairperson, Angela Hermitter, will officially start this evening's event."

Angela, her eyes shining, took the microphone from Glenn. "Thank you. As is customary, the baker whose cookies brought in the largest monetary donation last year is honored by his or her name added to the Bake Up a Cookie Storm honor roll on the wall there." She nodded toward a wooden plaque near the bar area.

Chad Trask, the owner of the café, gestured to it in the best television-hostess manner, producing laughter from the crowd.

"Thank you, Chad. I don't think Vanna has anything to worry about." The laughter continued until Angela held up the Gingerbread Drop she'd been holding and nodded toward Rona. "As if anyone here needs reminding, Rona Murray has the distinction of garnering that largest donation three years in a row. Is she about to make it four?"

Johnny bent to whisper in Rona's ear. "Angela sounds as if there's some doubt."

"She's just being a good emcee. Anyway, don't be too sure about the outcome of this, Johnny. There are a lot of talented bakers in town. Bidding could go sky high on anyone's donation."

"Yeah, well, I know some of these entrants' baking, and you've got nothing to worry about."

Rona's eyebrow rose as she stared at him. "And how do you know that?"

Johnny put his finger to his lips. "Angela's motioning to Chad."

"And, as is usual for our event, Chad Trask has graciously opened Dante's Café to us this evening. Such generosity deserves to be rewarded. Chad, would you like the first bite?" She held the cookie toward him, but he shook his head.

"I know how delicious they are." Chad patted his burgeoning stomach and sighed heavily. "Regrettably, I pass up the invitation. But thank you."

Angela curtsied and set her cookie on her napkin. "There's one other person who needs to be recognized for her hard work." She turned and motioned to a woman behind her. "Debbie Weingarten. Debbie, come up here."

Applause accompanied Debbie to the table.

"You don't see Debbie much because she's behind the scenes, contacting people for donations and then making sure the cookies get to the bidding tables. It's more work than you'd expect, and we couldn't do without her help. Thank you, Deb." Angela offered the tray of cookies to Debbie.

"Can I entice you, Chad, as thanks for this evening?" Debbie took a green frosted one and held it up for several seconds, perhaps waiting for the man to reply. He had his back turned slightly, talking to a woman next to him. When it was evident Chad was preoccupied, Debbie shifted her gaze to Glenn and bit into the cookie. "Delicious. You don't know what you're missing, Chad." Still chewing, she left the table area.

Johnny leaned closer to Rona and murmured, "Angela's got the mike again. She took a bite of your cookie. She's starting the auction. Do I bid now or wait until the last minute, building up the suspense as to the winner?"

Rona frowned. "I appreciate your support, but that doesn't get you off the hook. We'll talk about your knowledge of other women's baking later. Right now, you're saved by Angela's munch." She turned her attention to Glenn and Angela, then gripped Johnny's sleeve. "What…?"

Angela Hermitter looked like a bad imitation of The Mummy. She clutched Glenn and the edge of the cloth-covered table, and trembled slightly, as if she couldn't decide which way to turn. Her face contorted into a picture of pain. She lurched forward, bringing the tablecloth and the platters of cookies onto the floor. As she released her grip on the cloth, her hand went to her throat. Turning her face to one side, she bent over and lost her stomach.

Glenn stepped forward, his hands out to help her. As he waited for her sickness to stop, he pulled his cell phone from his phone and punched in 911. Seconds later, after relaying the information to the dispatcher, he picked up the microphone. "The ambulance is out on another run. It will be several minutes before one can be dispatched from Ste. Genevieve or Arnold." He glanced at Angela, now curled into a fetal position on the floor. "Even then, it'll be some time before it arrives. I think it best not to wait for help from the nearest town. If someone would give me a hand, we'll get her into my car, and I can meet the ambulance halfway. They can transport her to the hospital then. If someone will help me…" He didn't wait for a response but knelt beside Angela and wiped her face with his handkerchief.

Johnny rushed around to the far side of the tables. He slid his hands beneath Angela's arms and got her to her feet. Glenn grabbed the woman's legs as Chad supported her back. Someone opened the door, and they carried Angela outside and laid her in the back seat of Glenn's car. Johnny got into the passenger seat. "You concentrate on driving, Glenn. I'll keep an eye on Angela."

The man nodded, then tromped on the accelerator in his impatience. They zoomed off, leaving the café filled with rampant speculation and dozens of broken cookies.

Chapter Two

Back home and needing to bring a sense of normalcy to the horror she'd seen, Rona stood on her front porch. The temperature had fallen during the time she'd been at the café, and the wind had picked up, as though claiming the night hours as its habitation. It carried the clouds of her breath through the woods and into the night.

On other occasions she'd feel the cold, but she wasn't aware of it at the moment. A patch of moonlight lay at her feet, reminding her of the hour, yet she made no move to go inside. Unlike the chaos and anxiety of the past few hours, it was peaceful and calm here. And familiar. The river stretched out before her, black and mysterious. A rift in the clouds allowed another shaft of moonlight to crown the ridges of the river's waves with silver, creating a narrow band that connected the shores. The land, untouched by the moonlight, seemed to sleep in darkness. No lights shone other than the distant cell phone tower light that blinked its red alert on the Illinois side. No sounds disturbed the stillness other than the water lapping the beach and the lone call of an owl.

And a tugboat motor chugging from the river.

The sound was so familiar that she'd not been aware of it until the barges drew opposite her, but now it throbbed in her ears. She glanced up from staring at her feet to see the craft's running lights glide behind the tree trunks.

White, green and red. Like Christmas bulbs on a tree. Or colors thrown by stained glass onto the water, undulating and drawing the viewer into the mesmerizing depths. Deep colors did that, carried her back to her childhood, especially at Christmas.

Her home church had been an expansive pile of medieval architecture with Victorian *improvements*, and it had stood dark against many winters' whiteness. Doors and bell louvers closed as much against the elements as against burglary, and the building had always seemed a carcass silhouetted on its bleak hill. Yet, she recalled life within its stone walls: a glimpse of life called the traveler from the storm, the believer to the play. A whisper would slip occasionally from the tower shutters, the faint voice of a bell singing to Aeolus. A lancet window would glow with welcoming candlelight. Like a cat's eye in the darkness. Watching her journey across the frozen ground, assuring her of a sanctuary. The window danced within the solid black shape. Yellow, purple, blue, and red diamonds spilled onto the snow, their jeweled shapes stretching and convulsing as the candlelight behind the windows flickered.

Within the church walls, pine roping looped across pulpit and pews, scenting the cold air with hints of the season. Garlands of tiny silver bells twined among the greenery and hung from the wooden rafters and rear balcony. It was this church, this feeling she always remembered whenever she saw barge lights at night.

The tugboat horn sounded, and the memory vanished. She gazed at the river, the lights dancing, alive and mutely speaking of distant shores and adventures. Yet for some unexplainable reason, this time the lights were different. But for all that, the invisible bulk sliding through the blackness suddenly unnerved her. Like a giant red eye, the light on the port side slowly winked, as if it knew some dreadful secret. Near panic, she ran inside, the door banging behind her. She turned the dead bolt and hurried into the kitchen, where she heated up some apple cider, and took it into the back room.

It was a room that she identified most with her grandparents, shimmering like a mirage before her when she thought of the house. An open rectangle, the area sported a bay window that looked out into the woods. Floor-to-ceiling bookcases, in turn, flanked the window. The other walls showcased photographs and artwork by local artists. A couch sat at right angles to the wall, basking in front of the fireplace. She'd remodeled the entire room when she'd inherited the dwelling but left the grandeur of the ornate furniture and design to the dining and front rooms.

Still, for all her modernization of the back room, her grandparents occupied a place in this part of the house. They gazed, unsmiling and formal, from their tintypes on the fireplace mantle. Weather, hard work, and hard luck had shaped them, and they carried the results throughout their lives. Before her grandparents' birth, the locals had welcomed Rona's great grandparents to Klim, overlooking the Scottish brogue and their odd mannerisms. The local residents bonded through shared mishaps, individual joys, and simply trying to make a living, just as their great granddaughter Rona had. She'd been approved without reservation when she took up residence last year—some townsfolk even helped fix up the house and turn the barn into a bakery. Frontier days might be dead, but the old camaraderie of homesteaders remained. Her grandparents had unknowingly smoothed her acceptance into Klim.

An emphatic knock on the kitchen door startled her, and for a moment she envisioned some unknown figure from the dark barge standing on her stoop. She hurried into the kitchen and peeked outside. Seeing Johnny, she smiled and let him in.

Not knowing what to say, she draped his jacket over the back of a chair, and then poured him a cup of cider. As if sensing the conversation, once begun, was about to become serious, the CD of Christmas music ended. The sudden quiet filling the house was nearly as jolting as Angela's collapse had been.

"Glenn met up with the ambulance, I assume." Of course it was an inane thing to say, she thought, motioning Johnny to the kitchen table. He waited until she took a chair before sitting. "I mean, you wouldn't be back already if…" The sentence died as she gave up the pretense that Johnny had merely dropped by for a nightcap.

"Glenn drove around a bit. He was on the radio with the crew, trying to get closer to them for a swift transfer." He paused and took a sip, his gaze on her face, as if trying to discern how much to tell her. "Anyway, we caught up with them on North Main Street in Ste. Genevieve." His voice sounded tired, as if he'd carried Angela that entire thirty-five miles.

Rona frowned. Her hands wrapped tightly around the mug. "You didn't meet them halfway on the road somewhere?"

"Glenn had originally thought we could, but the ambulance was late leaving Ste. Gen. They didn't have to transport anyone, as they'd originally thought, but they gave the guy basic first aid and stayed to make sure he was alright before they left."

"Where'd they take her? To Arnold?"

Johnny shook his head and sagged against the back of the chair. His face looked pale and tired in the overhead light. "St. Louis has the nearest emergency facility. Even then…" He winced, setting his drink on the table. "We'd have been better off just driving her straight to the city. It's just a half hour's drive from Klim. But going to Ste. Genevieve, in the opposite direction, added miles and probably stretched the whole damned thing into two hours." The muscle in his jaw throbbed as he clenched his teeth in his apparent anger and inefficiency. "I'm no doctor, Ronnie, but she didn't look good."

"I can't imagine what's wrong with her. You saw her, Johnny. She was fine just before the auction began. Then she collapsed."

"Maybe we'll hear something tomorrow."

As if by signal, his cell phone rang. He pulled it from his pocket and glanced at the Caller ID display. "It's Glenn Somers."

"Maybe he has news…" Rona bit her bottom lip as Johnny answered the call.

"Hi, Glenn. Rona and I were just— What?" Johnny listened for several seconds, averting his gaze from Rona's face. Nodding, he rang off and laid the phone on the table. "That was Glenn," he said needlessly, rubbing the back of his neck.

"They must've made a diagnosis already, or he wouldn't have—"

"Rona, Glenn called with bad news. About the worst news anyone could hear." He paused, looking at her. The room fell deathly quiet. "Angela didn't make it. She died."

Rona set her mug on the table. Her eyes held the hurt that the loss of a close friend or family member produced. She opened her mouth, then paused, unsure of how to phrase her concern. "Dead! I can't believe it. Why? You rushed her to the ambulance. Surely they could do something for her while they drove to the hospital."

"She's dead, Rona. They got her to the hospital and did all they could, but she got there too late."

"But she was ill for just a few hours. What happened? That is, do they know yet how she—" She swallowed, staring at Johnny, silently pleading for an acceptable answer.

"Glenn said it's too soon to know yet."

"But it was a heart attack or something, right? I mean, she wasn't shot or stabbed, nothing obvious. She was sick, I guess. There's the vomit…" She broke off, her face drained of color. She pulled at the end of a strand of her hair, the red polish of her fingernails vivid in the kitchen light.

"There's the vomit, yes," Johnny said softly, as though easing the hurt. "It could mean a dozen different things, though. Glenn said he'll let us know when they have the postmortem examination finding."

Rona murmured her thanks and glanced out the window at the falling snow.

"I suppose, if there's any comfort in all this, it's that Angela had no children."

"She has a husband, though. That's just as bad, leaving someone who loved you." Rona talked more to the snow than to Johnny.

"That's tough. I don't envy Glenn Somers having to break the news to him. Do the Hermitters live around

Klim? I don't think I know. I've met Angela, of course."

"They live in town. On Arlington Drive."

"Near my gallery. Funny I've never seen him. Well, not that I'm aware of."

"You might not have. He's self-employed. Poor Steve." Rona ran the tip of her tongue across her lower lip. "Angela was always worried about him."

"Why's that? Does he have a dangerous job?"

"No. He spends a lot of time on the road. She was always concerned about drunk drivers and car accidents. Especially in rain or icy roads. Steve made a habit of phoning her whenever he arrived at a place and started back home. It eased Angela's mind."

"I think everyone in town will be eased once we know more about what killed Angela."

"I'm just sorry my cookie was the last thing she ate. It evidently ruined everything."

****

An hour later Rona walked Johnny to his car, her mind too full with Angela's tragedy to notice the wind pushing the falling snow onto her back. Johnny held her in his arms, as though keeping all the horrors of the event and the night-lurking creatures away from her, and then he kissed her.

She looked at him, trying to read his mind and heart, but he merely told her to get some sleep, and he'd phone her in the morning. The taillights of his Jeep disappeared over the rise of the hill before she could respond.

Inside, Rona leaned against the kitchen door. Even though she lived alone, the house suddenly felt empty, as though he'd taken its life and joy with him. She closed her eyes, breathing in the scent of his aftershave still lingering in the air, and wondered again if she should tell him her feelings.

She grabbed her cell phone, but her index finger hovered above the keypad. He might think she wanted him back only for comfort.

Giving it up as a bad idea, she locked the door and trudged to bed.

Chapter Three

Rona stood in her kitchen Saturday morning, sipping hot tea and gazing at the wintry world beyond the window. The river stretched from horizon to horizon, a wide, brown vein between the shores. Sunlight glanced off the watery surface, placid except for the eddy silently twisting near the beach below the hill. In warmer months she would stand on the gravel bar and listen to the waves lapping against the banks. The smell of wet mud and moss and the river itself stirred even now, alive in her nose and throat and mind. Mud, moss, and water—elements as ingrained in her memories of the Bar as they were of the river itself. Not until the flood had threatened to sweep her great grandparents' original cottage downstream did her grandparents abandon their residence and move to the spine of the hill. It was there they built the new house—even now, more than one hundred years later, it still stood solid and tall. Steep slopes bookended their patch of level lawn and woods, squeezed between the main Klim road to the west and the Mississippi River to the east. But they hadn't completely left their past behind. They could gaze down on the Bar, and the murky water, and conjure up ghostly images of the old cottage. The floor was nearly non-existent now, many wood planks rotted away or pilfered by others needing wood for bonfires or boating docks or lean-tos. Sand and mud splayed across the planking that was left, and some hardy plants poked through the gaps, their dry stalks rustling in the wind. The roof sheltered half of the dwelling, and consequently, offered no protection from the elements. What sunlight hadn't faded, the wind and rain had pounded into the dull wood. Yet, all the furniture, household items, and curtains had been safely moved up to the New House, leaving the old interior lifeless, but yet it still harbored those memories and ghosts.

Those days of barefoot visits were on hold, however, as Rona contended with the current December weather. On top of the bluff, where the great house sat, clumps of dried tufted, hairgrass poked out of the snowy drifts, their white plumes an autumnal memory, because long ago the biting wind had scattered the flower heads. Ferns and mums, once colorful, now nodded their drab brown stalks at her.

Snow coated the upper surfaces of tree branches and leaves, nestled between the wizened stalks of dead summer flowers, and topped the roof of the gazebo. Winter lay in the outcroppings of gray stone dotting the landscape where the wind had swept away snow. The woods surrounding her house stood out in stark relief, dark tree trunks against a white background. Her world was quiet, as if hibernating until spring. But she knew the feeling would soon fade as that morning's sunlight angled into the deeper regions of the woods. It was a pity—she loved the peace of twilight and early dawn.

A squirrel scampered across the lawn, leaving dimples in the smooth blanketing. Last night's storm hadn't lasted long…just long enough to cover the ground with three to four inches of white. Consequently, it hadn't taken much time to shovel a path from the kitchen door to the edge of the gravel parking lot beside her house.

The phone rang, jarring her from the memories of childhood visits. She grabbed her cell phone and smiled as Johnny's voice warmed her ear. "You're up early."

"Probably not compared to you. Did you sleep alright, Ronnie?"

"Not very. I kept thinking about…" She swallowed and wandered into the den. "Anyway, good morning, if that's not a crass thing to say."

"Glenn Somers called me a few minutes ago. He told me last night that he'd let me know when he found out anything, because we're…involved." He paused, as if waiting for Rona to say something.

"Was it a medical problem?" Rona took her hot tea to the couch and sat down. "I wasn't aware Angela had any concerns, but we didn't share intimacies over coffee, if you get what I mean."

"The postmortem exam said she died from poison."

Rona blinked, inhaling sharply. She tried to speak, but instead coughed.

"Are you okay, Ronnie?"

"Fine. I wasn't expecting that."

"Neither was Glenn."

"Is the hospital sure?"

"They double checked because the initial finding was so odd."

Rona's hand clutched her throat as she recalled Angela on the floor. "But poison! Angela didn't have an enemy in the world. She was beautiful, in body and in spirit. Everyone loved her."

"Evidently not *everyone*. Someone slipped the poison to her."

"What was it? Do they know yet?"

"Glenn said he should have that information a bit later. But the lab's certain it was poison."

Rona nodded, trying to understand it all.

Johnny cleared his throat, his voice hesitant and low. "Uh, Ronnie, I have to tell you that you're high on the suspect list."

"*Me?*" Her voice squeaked as she realized the impact of the sentence. "Why me? I liked Angela. We didn't quarrel."

"Maybe not in public, but Glenn has to investigate everyone connected with her."

"But he knows me. He knows I wouldn't harm anyone. Why am I on his suspect list?"

Johnny paused, as if not wanting to impart bad news. "Well, the last thing she ate was your cookie. Besides, knowing you doesn't make any difference with his investigation. He can't play favorites. You should realize that."

Rona leaned forward, her tea forgotten, and shook her head. "This makes no sense, Johnny. I didn't put anything in those Gingerbread Drops. Why would I?"

"I think that's one thing Glenn wants to talk to you about. He said something about hearing that you and Angela had had a falling out recently."

Her voice took on a sarcastic tone. "I wouldn't call it *recently*. It was two weeks ago. And it was over quickly. Hardly worth mentioning. He can't seriously think we were still…miffed."

Johnny groaned, and Rona could picture him running his fingers through his hair, as he usually did when frustrated. "I haven't a clue what the man thinks. He knows of it. And your recent falling out, coupled with the cookie she ate—"

"Right. Top of the Killer List. Great."

"Other people in town probably had motives too, sweets. I'm just telling you what Glenn told me."

"Thoughtful of him to warn me so I can buy my plane ticket to Brazil. Wonder if there's a red-eye flight…"

"Don't make jokes, Rona."

"If I don't, I might cry. Maybe I can help supply those other motives he'll need. Chad used to disappear for hours whenever she phoned him at the cafe."

"How do you know that?"

Rona exhaled, feeling as though she shouldn't have to explain. "I heard it from Paula. She works there."

"I'll let that pass, but the man's smart if he left. It doesn't pay to get mixed up with a married woman."

"And she had an on-going competition with her neighbor, Mike Heath. Baking, I think."

"County Fair and blue ribbons and such. I remember. I guess it can get pretty fierce when you're vying for the top purse. Baking with Clams, wasn't it?"

Rona rolled her eyes and shook her head. "No, Sugar. The competition was Baking with *Jams*."

"Clams…jams. Close. County Fair, 4-H… It's still a cooking contest. Who else is on your suspect list?"

"I don't like to include him, but how about hubby Steve?"

"Now you're definitely joking. They were happily married, Rona."

"To the world they were. But who knows what lurked beneath the surface?"

Johnny cleared his throat and murmured something before saying more loudly, "You sound like the beginning of that old time radio show *The Shadow*."

"Well, I wish *The Shadow* was around now. I'll want all the help I can get if I need to clear my name."

"Give Glenn time to investigate, Ronnie. The man's just started looking into this. He'll figure it out. Just relax."

Rona coughed, conveying her skepticism. "Relax, the man says. Relax in jail. I've been baking these cookies for decades, Johnny. It was one of the first recipes I ever made. I certainly think if I hadn't made a mistake as a ten-year-old, I surely wouldn't do anything wrong forty years later. And that includes adding poison."

"I guess there's always a first time, though what could've mistakenly got into the ingredients—"

"That's just it. Nothing unusual is in them. *Both* of us have eaten them, and we didn't get sick. It's just ordinary ingredients like flour, butter, cinnamon, molasses, walnuts... Anyway, what's Glenn think happened? Could Angela have had an allergic reaction?"

Johnny muttered that he had no idea, but she wouldn't have eaten cookies if she were. "Eggs are in just about all baked goods, aren't they?"

Rona continued as if Johnny hadn't spoken. "I double-checked the ingredients before I refrigerated the dough. I made certain I didn't forget anything. There was no sink scouring powder or plant food on the kitchen counter. I can't imagine that anything was wrong with my recipe. There has to be another source of the poison. Maybe something she ate for lunch, and it just reacted hours later, at Chad's, during the cookie auction."

"Well, that's for Glenn to find out. Maybe he can question the person who made the drinks."

"What about her husband, or a former boyfriend? Or a neighbor? Isn't Glenn going to question them?"

"Sure, he will, but right now—"

"Yes." Rona exhaled loudly, needing to release her anxiety. "I'm tops on his list."

"The husband, Steve, got to the hospital after I left last night. Glenn had phoned him so he could be with her."

"If he didn't arrive until after you left, why was he so late?"

"I have no idea."

"I've not seen him much around town. Our schedules don't seem to coincide."

"Well, I've never met him. According to Glenn, Steve was very distraught last night."

Rona stood up, the phone jammed between her ear and shoulder. "I should think he would be. From the little I knew, he loved her very much."

"She seemed like a nice person."

"Well, I'm not going to wait to be questioned, Johnny. I've had enough trouble with false accusations. I don't want another one ruining my bakery business. I'm just rebounding from the latest round of gossip. This isn't going to be another launch pad for scandal."

Johnny's voice was laced with wariness. "Ronnie, what are you going to do?"

"Do a bit of investigating on my own, beginning with people who attended the auction last evening. I'm going to make sure my name stays untarnished. And there won't be any crumbs left for rumormongers to sink their teeth into."

Chapter Four

Debbie Weingarten looked up from scattering breadcrumbs for the birds as Rona parked in front of the woman's house. A slight breeze fanned Debbie's shoulder-length hair around her face and carried the clouds of her frozen breath into the trees. She tilted the pie plate, emptying it of the last crumbs, and squinted into the sunlight. Recognizing Rona, she gave a weak smile. "Morning. I'm not calling it good, not after yesterday's tragedy, but it's nice to see you." Debbie swept her hand across the plate's surface and knocked it against the porch railing to discharge any stubborn last bits. "You have time for coffee?"

Rona picked up a chunk of bread that had fallen onto a holly branch and tossed it near the majority of the crumbs on the snow. "That sounds nice, thanks."

Debbie nodded and preceded Rona up the front walk. The house seemed to be a living topiary bush, Rona thought, for boxwood roping festooned the tops of the windows and porch columns, and a pine and yew swag concealed most of the door.

The home's interior mimicked the exterior, with roping, swags, and a mammoth Christmas tree occupying most of the space in the living room. The scent reminded Rona of a forest except for the absence of twittering birds.

They hung up their jackets and wandered into the

kitchen, where Debbie poured two mugs of coffee and motioned Rona to a chair at the table. She laid a fern-colored napkin at Rona's place, then sat down. "You here for a specific reason, or just dropped by to commiserate about Angela?"

"Angela. Not that it's not nice to chat with you, Debbie."

"No need to apologize. She was pretty sick last night. How is she? Have you heard?"

"Yes. Unfortunately, she died last night."

Debbie eased her mug onto the table, then wrapped her arms over her chest, staring at Rona with pain-filled eyes. "Dead! You—you can't be serious."

"It's true. We learned last night."

"But how can that be? Did she have a heart attack?"

"We may find out later, but they think it was…something she ate."

"Food poisoning?" Debbie shook her head, and her fingertips dug into her upper arms. "It's unbelievable. Angela gone. Poor Steve. How he must be hurting. To lose someone like that…" As if to underscore her statement, the limb of a pine tree knocked against the house and discarded the snow laced among its needles. "I suppose he'll marry again…in time, I mean, but he'll grieve for a while. I know he loved Angela. Well, we all did. But he doesn't strike me as the sort of guy who can live single. Many men aren't like that." She grabbed a tissue from the box on the table and dabbed at her eyes. "I'll call a few people. We can trot some casseroles and things over to him. I doubt if he'll feel like cooking." She sniffed and balled the tissue in her hand. "I just can't believe all this. It's…so unbelievably sad."

"It's bad, yes. You were with Angela at the auction.

Did anything strike you odd? Maybe not at the time, but thinking about it now?"

"What do you mean odd?"

Rona picked up her coffee mug but held it on her lap. "I don't know. You and she were in the kitchen for a while. Maybe she exchanged words with someone, or she mentioned not feeling well."

"Why are you asking? Isn't this something the police should be doing?" Debbie's eyes narrowed, as though she was sizing up Rona's reason for her visit. "You wouldn't be trying to find out what I heard or saw, would you?"

"Why would I do that?"

"So you'll know if anyone saw your actions."

Rona nearly choked on her coffee. "You can't mean it. What actions do you think I need to cover up? I came into the kitchen with Johnny. I gave you the boxes of cookies. I stood not two feet from you as we chatted for a few minutes, then Johnny and I left. So how am I supposed to have done anything to Angela?"

Debbie pursed her lips together and shook her head. "I'm sorry, Rona. I didn't mean anything by it." Her voice was flat, as though Angela's death had sucked the life from her too. She opened her mouth, closed it, then opened it again as she stroked a strand of her hair. "Sorry, it's just that... Well, this whole thing is so— I don't know. So unreal. I talked to Angela at the auction, and this morning you tell me she's gone." Her hand slid down to the buttons of her sweater, her fingers feeling them like worry beads. "I was just trying to explain her death in my own clumsy way. Sorry."

"That's alright. Her passing will upset a lot of people." Rona set her mug on the ceramic coaster featuring a graphic of a snowy pine branch. The colors blended well with the similar kitchen scheme. "So, you didn't see or hear anything last evening. Angela didn't say anything bothered her."

"No. We talked about the usual things. Well, you know the conversations never seem to vary from auction to auction. Which person brought what? Do we have any new entrants? Whose cookie will probably bring in the highest bid... Things like that." Debbie abandoned the buttons as she shrugged and leaned back in her chair, eliciting a squeal from the furniture's old joints. "There wasn't anyone in the kitchen who shouldn't have been there, either. It was just the usual folks from the committee."

"When I brought in my donation, I saw you, Angela and Glenn. Anyone else there?"

"Chad, of course, but it's his café. Anyway, he didn't do anything. Just came back every so often...to see if..." Her last statement came out piecemeal, the words slightly shaky. "You know...see if everything was all right."

Which it hadn't been, Rona thought as she left.

Chapter Five

Chad Trask, owner of Dante's Café, had finished breakfast but was lingering over his cup of coffee when Rona arrived at his house. The house looked as though *it* was still surviving the news of last evening's sad incident. The living room curtains were partially open; his jacket was sprawled across the couch; and a plate, glass, and mug sat on the coffee table. He picked up the newspaper from the floor and let it drift onto a chair.

"It's a Gunfire if you want to know the truth." He held up the cup containing the mixture of hot, black coffee and rum, then asked, "You want one?"

"No, but thanks for the offer."

"I'm not apologizing for the drink. I need it." He downed a long swallow before motioning her to the couch. A sharp wind rose, blowing across the lawn with a moan as it raced between the houses on Chad's street. Now it threw pellets of sleet against his living room windows. Chad apparently didn't hear it. "My apology for peering out the window at you when you were at the door, but I wanted to make sure you weren't Debbie. Please, take a seat."

Rona wandered over to the indicated piece of furniture and sat down.

"You know I'm not a big drinker, Rona, and I certainly don't drink in the morning. But after last night…" He winced and sagged onto the cushions. A slant of sunlight fell across his forehead and the side of his face, illuminating small furrows and the dullness of his eyes. He ran his fingers through his hair, further mussing the already untidy dark mass. Sighing, he tilted his head back and gazed at the ceiling. "What a horrible evening. Winter event or not, nothing like that's ever happened at my place. I hope she's better this morning."

"Unfortunately, no. She passed last night."

Chad said something under his breath and stared into the cup. His jaw dropped, and he suddenly looked older. "I'm sorry to hear that. Steve must be going through hell. They were very close. I know he'll miss her. The whole town will." He downed the last of his drink and set the cup on the side table. "I guess it's too soon to know about any…you know…service. To bury her, I mean."

The phrase joggled another one in her mind. Burying a dead man. An old boating term.

Rivermen would pound a log vertically into the riverbed to create a mooring site. There were two ancient docking posts still standing along her stretch of the Mississippi. The wood, bleached bone-white, was hard as sinew and probably a remainder of many that had been beaten in long ago by river pirates, traders, and flatboatmen. But most had been washed away or uprooted for use as dock or house lumber.

They buried the post ends six feet down, sinking them into the sand, mud, and soil, leaving the upper six feet of log standing clear of the water. Rivercraft would tie-on, a necessity in rural or flood-prone regions with unreliable or non-existent docking spots. Too often trees at the shoreline proved insecure, for their roots became exposed by weather and time, and eventually would crash into the river. The dead man could be trusted.

Chad cleared his throat, knocking the scene from Rona's mind. She shook her head. "I doubt if Steve's had time to think about any service, Chad."

"Right." He nodded and gazed at the wall clock.

The ticking seemed to fill the room, Rona thought, sounding like a heartbeat measuring the moments of a life.

"Obviously, I don't know about her health…" Chad's comment broke into Rona's contemplation. "But she always seemed strong to me. I've never known her to have a cold, let alone anything major." He paused and shifted his position on the couch, his face falling into the gloom of the room. "Not that I knew personal details, but I'd see her around town at least once a week. And she and Steve would have a meal or drink in the café about that often. She seemed… well…fine." His fingers swept through his hair again, rearranging the short spikes. "I guess that's part of what makes this so tragic, her dying so suddenly."

"Part of it is shock, yes. I guess I saw her slightly less often than you. I'm sorry I didn't know her better."

"I remember once…oh, a few years ago…she asked my opinion about the feasibility of opening a bakery."

"Really?"

"This was a few years before you moved to Klim, Rona."

"If I'd known her heart was with baking instead of writing, I wouldn't have opened my bakery."

Chad shook his head, giving her a half smile. "I think she wasn't that serious. She just wanted information about regulations and what she could expect for weekly income and prices of renovating useable shops. As much as she likes to bake, I know her first love was writing."

"I wonder why she considered switching careers. Her books sell, don't they?"

"Who knows why she had thoughts of opening a shop. I'd say to get away from Steve, but from what I hear, they had a great marriage. Besides, there are easier ways to put some space between you and your spouse than running a business. That's a hell of a lot of work."

Rona nodded, envisioning her own bakery. "If that was her motive for looking into owning a business, I'd be surprised. She already had lots of alone time with Steve gone on his route for days."

"Maybe her life *was* rough when he was home. I never heard, but who knows what goes on behind closed doors."

"I hope that wasn't the case. He may have come home angry at customers and taken it out on her. But if it were true, now I hope he regrets how he treated her."

Chad chewed on his bottom lip, his focus on the floor. In the quiet, the sound of the refrigerator kicking on brought back a tinge of everyday life to the surreal topic of Angela's death. The noise seemed to jolt him from his contemplation.

He stretched and stared at Rona, then after a few seconds, asked, "I don't mean to appear rude, but is this why you stopped by? I haven't talked to Debbie, thank God, or the other committee members, but I'd think we'll try for another fundraiser in the spring, after everyone's had a chance to…get over this."

"That sounds great. You could call it A Shower of Cookies if you hold it in April. Or…anything else," she added hurriedly, realizing she wasn't on the fund-raising board. "Sorry."

"No, no, don't apologize. I'll toss that into the ring when the group gets together." He hesitated, pulling at his ear lobe. "Are you interested in joining?"

Rona blinked at the invitation. "Sorry?"

"With Angela...gone...we have a vacancy. We'll need another committee member. You have a lot of good ideas, Rona. You're extremely creative. Would you consider helping out?"

"It's not that I don't want to, Chad, but I have all I can handle with the bakery and running the events center."

"Sure. Besides, if you're a committee member, you can't enter your cookies in the auction."

"Other entrants might appreciate that. Oh, dear. That sounded like I expect to continue winning next year. I didn't mean—"

"I won't tell anyone. Don't worry." He gave her a half smile before his face fell serious.

"You'd better think of someone else, Chad. I won't have the time to give to the group. Thank you anyway."

He nodded, raising his right hand in a half-hearted acknowledgment before letting it fall back to his lap. "At least we always know your word is good, whatever you say. Unlike...some." The words were tinted with frustration.

Rona started to reply, but Chad continued, "Marriage doesn't solve problems. I realize that. But sometimes I wish I had a ring on my finger. It'd solve one female problem I have." The corner of his mouth contorted as he snorted. "Do you know anyone who could play a convincing minister or a bride? No, that won't work. I should go to an acting agency for people.

I suppose those are still in existence…" He steepled his fingers, tapping the tips together. "Why does life have to be so complicated? Why can't we just live and let live? Poor Angela…"

Rona pressed her lips together, uncertain what to say.

A dog barked somewhere outside before Chad spoke again. "Sorry. Pay me no mind. It's just the shock of all this." He glanced at his wristwatch. "Enough, I've got to get on with my day. As I said, I don't mean to be rude, but I really haven't time for all this."

"I'll leave in a minute. I just want to know if you saw anything unusual last night."

He frowned, leaning forward and eyeing her with what looked like suspicion. His tone was sharp, conveying annoyance or fright. "What do you mean unusual? I know you have a history of getting involved in mysteries, shall we call it, but frankly, I find your playing at Sherlock Holmes rather gruesome under the circumstances. I'd think you'd let Glenn Somers and the rest of the police department handle this. You're under no suspicion that I know of. And there's nothing suspicious about Angela's death, other than it being unexpected and dramatic. No one skulked around the café. No one wore a black trench coat and sunglasses. I'm not making light of her death, but you're overdramatizing this, Rona. Leave it for Glenn and the professionals." He stood up, grabbing his cup. "Now, sorry to shoo you out, but I have to get dressed and get to the café. Hopefully, I'll be able to salvage part of the day and open later. That's if anyone's brave enough to venture into the house of death."

Chapter Six

Angela's neighbor, Mike Heath—a mid-30s pillar of strength with a take-charge voice—didn't know about any stranger who'd visited her recently. He must have thought Rona needed more elucidation, for he added that he *did* know that there had been no unfamiliar cars parked outside the Hermitter home yesterday morning.

A haze of stubble covered his chin and matched the general unkempt air of his clothing, and though the holes in his jeans might have been part of the current fashion trend, the smudges on his sweater spoke of indifference or work. He picked up a sprig of yew that had fallen from the wreath on his front door and inserted it back into the greenery. "Sorry. Don't mean to freeze you," he said, closing the door, but not before the aromas of pine, damp moss, and wood smoke twined inside. "It's pathetic, but if I don't do it now, I'll forget. I normally come and go via the garage." He brushed his hands against his jeans, his gaze on her. "Who'd have thought it'd be so cold in December."

"Or so snowy. Maybe those persimmons are right."

"I don't doubt anything that nature tells us. Now, you must want to know about Angela. Other than those cars of hers and her husband's, I mean," he added after Rona took a seat in his living room. It reflected the major accomplishments and adventures of his life, he said when he found Rona gazing at a framed photo of a hummingbird sipping nectar from a petunia. "I got an award for that. One of my better shots."

Rona murmured that the sunlight on the bird's throat and wings was striking.

"I was lucky to get such a good angle, and that my garden was at its peak."

"It looks like it, if the rest of your pictures are any indication." She gazed at the other photos of flowers and birds.

"Two of my passions." His voice rose as he spoke more quickly. "I like birds because a really good shot is hard to catch, and I like my plants due to the colors and textures. I'm partial to hostas and liriope. They can't be beat if you want to define or fill in a large space. I accent that with staples like hollyhocks, roses, larkspur, and lilies, then throw in creeping phlox and daisies. I spend a lot of time planning and tending to it, which is why I couldn't believe Debbie this past spring when she told me she'd torn out half of her garden. Said she would be starting from scratch this next year. But the older plants tend to need replacing. Still…all that work!"

"Is that why you have those small bowls of seeds on your windowsill?"

He turned to look at them, as though not seeing the containers before. "Sure. I save them from year to year. Then I can sow new plants when they're needed. That's what keeps life interesting, isn't it? Like all of my travels." He gestured toward the photos of tropical beaches, Bali temples, and Venetian canals that dotted his walls.

Rona let the topic lapse before saying, "I guess you heard about Angela."

"Yeah. I phoned Steve this morning. If I'd known

she'd passed, I wouldn't have bothered him." Mike broke off. He tapped his fingers against his lips, frowning, his face draining of color. "What a tragedy. She was as pretty as she was intelligent. I can't imagine she was ill."

"Did Steve mention she was poisoned?"

"Poisoned!" His voice held a mixture of disbelief and horror. "No. He never said a word. Are you sure? Is that what the police said?"

"That's what the hospital postmortem report stated."

"How could she have been poisoned?" He stared at her, his eyelashes casting shadows on his cheeks. "I can't believe it was suicide. She had so much to live for. She was excited about her work. She had no reason to end her life. That's absurd."

"I think the police have to investigate, Mike. It might've been an accident."

"I suppose it could be. Still, it's an awful shock for us, and an awful way to die."

Wanting to lighten the mood, Rona asked if he had other items from his travels.

"Some." A tinge of exasperation laced his words, as though the subject was too trivial in light of Angela's tragedy. He exhaled deeply, his fingers drumming on the arm of the chair. "I've displayed only these things you see here. Angela got a kick out of seeing my stuff, you know, but Steve really asked a lot of questions. Neither of them traveled much. Well, apart from Steve traveling for his work, I mean. I suppose they couldn't go on long trips, on account of their jobs. His sales position kept him driving around a lot, and Angela was pretty much glued to her desk most of the time. If she wasn't working on a new book, she was chin-deep in edits. That's what she was engrossed with at the moment, the editing deadline of her current book manuscript. But they enjoyed hearing about my adventures, and they seemed content with long weekend jaunts. Debbie Weingarten too. She and I used to go together for a time, did you know?" His voice lowered and sounded annoyed. "It was fine until she turned into a leech. I dated Angela briefly too, when she and Steve were separated, but they got back together." His voice became lighter as he evidently abandoned painful memories. "Anyway, Debbie saw my collection when she and I were chummy. She had a ton of questions about native flora and fauna. I was glad to tell her, glad to share my interest. I think that's what initially drew us close."

Rona cut him off to ask if he had heard anything yesterday near Angela's house.

"*Heard* anything?" He blinked rapidly. "Like what? What time?"

"I don't know. Before she left for Chad's café to emcee the cookie auction. Did you hear or see anyone at her door, or a cry for help? Was Steve home yesterday?"

He settled back in his chair, and scratched his jaw, simultaneously looking mad and ill at ease. His fingers tapped the end of the armrest, and he briefly closed his eyes, perhaps to picture the driveway. When he opened them again, they were dark with regret. "Steve wasn't due home until early evening. At least, if he kept to his schedule, he wouldn't have been early. But as to hearing anyone there… No. Nothing at all."

"No one came to the house? Friend, delivery van…"

"Not that I saw. Of course, they could've come and gone after I left for work, which I did at nine. I got to the office thirty minutes later. It's in south St. Louis." He paused, frowning, as though he dared Rona to phone his boss. "I suppose someone could've dropped by then. I left there at normal quitting time, around five, and got home close to five forty. Then I ate and got to Chad's just before the shindig began at seven. I'm sorry. Not much use, am I?" He shook his head, seeming to silently chastise himself. "I'd like to help. I liked her. It's bad enough to die, but like she did…" He slumped down in his chair.

"Did Angela have any history of trouble?"

"What, like burglaries? I can't believe a burglar would've poisoned her."

"Not a burglary. I mean domestic violence," Rona suggested when he looked puzzled. "And I'm not suggesting between her and Steve. Any problem with a friend or an on-going battle with a local company?"

"If she did have trouble with Steve, they kept it quiet from everyone. She moved to Klim about…what? Fifteen or so years ago? That's ample time for the word to get around that they were having problems. *IF* they did." He shook his head, mutely underscoring his opinion. "I should think the police would know, though. Or her minister."

Rona nodded, wondering if she was getting in deeper than was healthy. "So, you didn't see anyone suspicious yesterday. Or see any friend's car, especially if it was at an odd hour."

"Like, John Doe comes over at noon on Mondays and Thursdays, but yesterday he stopped by at nine?" Mike snorted. "Doesn't follow. But she did have her usual breakfast companion yesterday."

Rona held up his hand. "Pardon? *What* usual breakfast companion? Do you know her?"

"I should think so. I've seen him around often enough."

"*Him?*"

"Sure. At seven-thirty. And it's not just at breakfast he drops by, either. He's been over many times, all hours, though mainly in the late afternoons, right before he has to get to work. Steve's never home at that time, which is kind of weird." Mike drew in the corner of his mouth, looking at Rona as though he was trying to read her mind. "Why? Is something wrong? He's been over so much lately, and nothing has happened to her, and then seeing him other times... Well, I didn't think anything strange was going on."

"The *name*, Mike."

"What? Oh, it's Chad Trask."

Chapter Seven

Rona was sitting in her car, thinking of whom to talk to next, when Johnny phoned. She leaned against the back of the car seat, the phone nestled against her ear, and stared at Mike's house. Icicles fringed a section of the front gutter and dripped sporadically as they melted.

"Just checking on you, Ronnie."

"I'm a big girl, Johnny. All I'm doing is talking to people."

"You talked to people about those other incidents you got embroiled in, and it nearly cost us our lives in September. Or do you have selective memory?"

"My memory's fine, thanks. No one's going to offer me poisoned tea, so you don't have to gallop over on your white horse, though I appreciate your concern." She angled her body into the corner created by the car seat and the door and breathed deeply. The car held the scents of last evening's cookies and Johnny's aftershave. She told him about Chad's visits to Angela.

"So, you think they were having an affair?" Johnny's voice sailed into Rona's ear, warming her.

"From Mike's comment, it could be. Chad seems to have been over more often than would warrant fixing her faulty plumbing. *And* over when Steve wasn't home. I don't like slandering people, Johnny, but if you have a more plausible explanation, I'm ready for a suggestion."

Johnny mumbled that he was working on it,

although nothing seemed to suggest itself at the moment. "I don't know Chad very well, but could he be writing a book and needing her help?"

"Something on the order of *Ninety-nine Bottles of Beer on the Wall, or How to Own a Café*? It's possible, but Chad doesn't strike me as the literary type."

"Just an idea, Rona. So why was Chad at Angela's home all those times? Maybe more importantly, why was he there yesterday morning?"

"Need I remind you that we have only Mike's word for these assignations?"

He murmured she was right. "I don't know why, but if Mike's correct about Chad, I'm disappointed in the man. I thought he was upstanding. And I can't imagine him popping over so they could feed each other donut holes."

"*Someone* had to have been there if it's…" She paused, suddenly afraid to voice her thought.

"If it's murder, is what you're thinking. I can't believe her death is an accident either, but of course the police will figure that out."

"Still, Johnny, it seems the only logical explanation. You saw the auction and you were there when the EMTs picked her up last evening. You'd know. Her symptoms are certainly indicative of poisoning, and we have the postmortem findings."

"The police will know that. Hold on. I've got a call. I'll phone you right back if it's Glenn."

Rona nodded, ended the call, and waited in the car. Johnny's voice still echoed in her ear, its tone warming her. She glanced again at the house and street, and suddenly felt as desolate as the landscape. Desolate *and* alone, she appended. Alone and lonely. She was certain now her divorce had been a mistake. And, if she were truthful, she could use the stability his height and demeanor suggested. Nothing ruffled his feathers. That had irritated her in the early months of their marriage, for she had misread that as disinterest on his part. But now she realized it was his calm disposition and his ability to think through any upheaval.

She pressed her lips together, forcing the blood from them, and stared again at the houses on the street. Many people in town had already formed opinions about her involvement in Angela's death, the incident that mimicked several previous deaths that had nearly enveloped her. And her grandmother's words sounded as loudly in her mind as if the older woman were standing there. "Tongues wag mercilessly when there's even a shadow of a possibility of anything to be gossiped about. Scandal and tragedy oil the jawbones. And those jawbones waggle best in a small town where nothing seems to happen. Smilers pounce on a morsel and turn it into a feast, and eyes watch for you to fall on your fanny. Grist for gossip's never far off. And there doesn't need to be any truth for its foundation." Well, I'm not hiding from the gossip, she thought. I'm clearing my name before Glenn Somers has a chance to formally question me.

She'd just talked herself into going to his office and telling him what she'd learned, when her phone rang. "I assume that was Glenn with more information," she replied to Johnny's "Hello."

"He wanted to let me know about the other test results that came in."

"Should I skip town now or am I free to walk around?"

"I think you can tiptoe around, though you aren't completely clear of suspicion until he learns how the poison was administered."

"Has he figured out if it's an accident, at least?"

"By her own hand, you mean? He didn't sound like it, Ronnie. He's certain of time of death merely because he was with Angela at the hospital."

"So, the cell doors can still clank closed on me."

"Will you wait to hear the whole thing before you start packing your orange jumpsuit?"

"Sorry. Proceed."

"Well, the burning in her mouth and the vomit she had are some of the symptoms of larkspur poisoning. The ambulance attendant said her heartbeat continued to slow on the way to the hospital. Not very pleasant."

Rona started to reply, then thought better of it. She stared out the car window. The snow flurries of earlier morning had nearly stopped, though slushy drops still plopped sporadically onto freezing puddles dotting the road. A squirrel paused on the limb of an oak, perhaps judging how wet he'd get if he ventured onto the lawn.

"Did you hear me, Rona?"

She nodded slowly. "How did she get larkspur? Mistakenly taking an overdose of something, I can understand, but *larkspur*? The flower's not even growing now."

"You've found out a lot that Glenn will want to know, but I think you should stop now. If it's murder, you don't need to be involved in this."

"Did Glenn say anything about…still thinking I'm involved? Aside from Angela eating my cookie and then getting sick, it's well known in town that I do like to garden."

Johnny groaned. "So do a hundred other people, Ronnie. That doesn't necessarily point the finger at you. Anyway, I can't see how you're supposed to have introduced larkspur into your cookie. Or gotten her to eat it. That's beyond belief."

Rona asked hesitantly, "Is he having the rest of the Gingerbread Drops analyzed?"

"If he is, I'm getting you a lawyer. Why would you risk killing Angela, if she was your intended victim, in front of everyone with an entire batch of poisoned cookies? You had no idea who would buy those things at the auction." He stopped abruptly, and the silence over the phone screamed at Rona.

"Even though *you* would've probably been the high bidder," she added, her voice barely audible.

"Which brings us back to the question of motive and the actual target. Unless you've turned into a spree killer, you wouldn't have known for certain who'd end up with the cookies." He exhaled loudly. "I don't believe any of it. Not your premeditation or thrill from killing an innocent person."

"Thank you. It's nice to know someone believes me innocent."

"Lots of folks do."

"Well, I still have to talk to lots of folks. If Glenn considers me the prime suspect, especially after the larkspur finding, I need to find out who doctored my food, if that's how it was done, although it could've been something she ate at home before she left for the auction. Or even in her drink. Do you remember what Angela was drinking at the café?"

"Why don't you ask me something easy, Rona, like who'll win the World Series next year? I have no idea

85

what she drank, but it had a cinnamon stick or something similar sticking out of the mug. You could ask Chad or one of the people she talked to last evening. They might remember."

"One of the others! Thanks for reminding me. I nearly forgot about her minister."

"Hold on a minute. Let's talk about all this over lunch. How's that sound?"

"I really don't want to spend the time. No offense. If Glenn's honing in on me—"

"Rona, we're having lunch. You can't do all this on nervous energy. Where do you want to go?"

Silence answered him.

"Rona, I'm serious. *Lunch.* Where?"

"Okay. But let me talk to Angela's minister first. If I don't, I'll forget."

"All right, but he's the only person. Where do I meet you?"

"Well, I'd suggest the café, but under the circumstances, you better come to my house. I've got some soup and I can probably find something for sandwiches."

"Fine. See you when you get there."

"*Ora pro nobis.*" She switched on the motor, and eased the car away from the curb, hoping the clergyman might shed some divine insight into Angela's relationships.

Chapter Eight

There was nothing particularly colorful about the church. It stood as a dark mass nestled among equally dark trees and against the white landscape. It was probably lively and colorful in the spring, or magical with Christmas Eve candlelight, but now it was merely a quiet building. Driving back home an hour later, Rona remembered the rustle of the wind stirring everything not nailed down. The red bow, starched from sleet and frozen overnight, stood crisply on the south door. A sprig of holly looked already defeated by Nature's blast, for it sagged in the bow's knot. Below it, as though shaken by the force of the door's closing, several berries dotted the snow, blood red drops on white.

Back home, she and Johnny talked over their broccoli and cheddar soup. No, the minister had said as Rona stood in the nave of the church—a lumber-clad, cross-shaped area that smelled of pine and recently polished wood and candle wax. And echoed from their speech. No, Angela Hermitter had not confided in him about any problems in her life, beyond the fact that her last few years had been rather rough at times due to Steve's passion for football. Nor had Angela unloaded any more recent troubles on his wife, and his wife would have told him, deeming it better to lose a friend than for that friend to lose her life. Yes, Angela and Steve had been model church members, giving of their time, talents, and tithes. No, he hadn't heard of Angela's passing until Rona had informed him—he hadn't been able to attend the cookie auction last evening. It was a terrible, shocking thing that drained the color from his face and prodded a murmur of 'Dear God' from his lips. Yes, he would hurry over to offer what he could to the poor, grieving husband. No, he didn't know of anyone who wished Angela ill, unless Rona considered her sporadic feud with the butcher a likely scenario. Nor did he know of any medical problem she had. His wife would have nagged Angela into seeing the doctor if she'd known. No, he didn't know of any former boyfriends who might cause trouble. Yes, it would surprise him to learn of an adulterous affair, but such things happened these days, didn't they?

"So much for clerical confessions," Rona said, scraping the last of the soup from her bowl.

"You weren't having a confession. Wrong religion, I think. Anyway, he wasn't going to divulge anything to you. No offense, Ronnie, but you're not the police. He didn't want to tell anything titillating to an ordinary resident. Glenn will find out more later when he speaks to people."

"Yes, well, the minister could've been a tad more helpful. I don't know anything more now than before I talked to him."

"You know Angela and the butcher didn't get along."

"Funny. I hardly think fatty pork chops or a heavy thumb on the meat scale constitutes such customer anger that the butcher would retaliate by murder, Johnny."

"Just a suggestion, sweets. Keep an open mind. By the way, I didn't get a chance to tell you the last bit of info from Glenn. When the lab ran the blood toxicology test, they came up with alkaloid—the toxic ingredient in larkspur."

"I still find this terribly hard to believe. How did Angela consume that?"

"Haven't the foggiest. Did I tell you the police found two used cups and dessert plates in the kitchen sink?"

"At Angela's home?"

Johnny stretched and yawned, then apologized. "Late night. Well, you know. Anyway, Glenn suspects they're left from earlier yesterday, like she had someone over and they left the cups and plates there because she had to leave for the auction. The food remnants are very dry."

Rona paused, thinking. "I wonder if Chad had tea and donut holes with Angela before they left, and if so, maybe he put the poison into her tea."

"I'm afraid it's a bit more serious than that."

"More serious than donut holes?" She angled her head, trying to judge what he was going to say. "What?"

Johnny ran his fingers through his hair, wincing. "I hate to tell you…"

"The sound of your voice tells me. I have a feeling I should pack my orange jumpsuit."

"The police found one of your bakery cartons on the kitchen counter. Empty."

The implication seemed to scream at Rona in the quiet of the room.

"Except for some crumbs," Johnny added, his eyes dark.

"And the police think the poison was in whatever they ate from my bakery? That's absurd!" Her voice shook as she got to her feet.

Johnny's hand clamped around her wrist and forced her back into her chair. "Don't jump to conclusions, Ronnie. I don't know what the police think. That carton could've been there since last week."

"Angela kept a tidy house."

"I'm using that as an example. Perhaps she and her breakfast partner didn't eat anything at all. She and Steve could've had your bakery product a day ago. After all, he's all right. That carton's just clutter."

"Well, they obviously ate *something* if there are two dirty dishes there. She had to ingest the larkspur with some food. She wouldn't guzzle them just out of a bowl."

"I suppose someone did eat something. But just because Mike didn't see anyone over there doesn't mean there wasn't someone. He was at work most of the day, anyway."

Rona snapped her fingers, speaking more quickly. "Could *he* have been seeing her? He said they were boyfriend/girlfriend at one time."

"Didn't she and Steve get married fifteen years ago? That's an awful long time to still be jealous or desirous."

"Johnny, my dear innocent lamb, when does marriage to one preclude dalliance with another? Maybe they still had feelings for each other."

"I suppose so. And you said she and Steve dated others during their separation."

"If Mike was still interested in her, could he have poisoned Angela's tea and conveniently failed to mention to me that he'd been over there, and therefore incriminated Chad?"

"Even if they weren't an item anymore, maybe there's another motive for the killing. Had they fallen out over something else?"

Rona's voice took on a hint of skepticism. "You mean a neighborly thing? Like what? Yapping dog? Grass mowing? Late to bring in the garbage cans?"

"That's usually the stuff of residential disputes, Rona. Don't poo-poo the idea."

"Mike mentioned he'd been seeing Debbie Weingarten for a while. I don't know how serious that was, but it evidently petered out. I can't see a motive in any of this for Mike killing Angela. If only we knew whose DNA was on that second cup and plate. That could have been when she was poisoned."

"It'll be nice if it proves to be true, but unfortunately things don't always turn out the way we wish." He spoke slowly, as though there was another meaning behind his words.

"Shoving me and my Gingerbread Drops into Glenn's spotlight again."

"Even so, *if* it was in the cookie and not the drink, the killer was still taking a chance poisoning your cookie. Sure! Do you remember the beginning of the auction?"

"How can I forget? You mentioned you knew some other women in town who could bake really—"

"Not that, Rona. Angela stood at the table, talking into the microphone. She offered the cookie to Chad." Johnny paused, giving her a chance to catch up to his conclusion.

Rona nodded, her breathing becoming more rapid in her excitement. "Right! I'd forgotten. She made some to-do about letting him have the first cookie because he'd let us use the café."

"Right. But he lets her have the honor…or, as it turned out, the mouthful of poison."

Rona chewed her bottom lip as she thought through

the scenario. Her voice took on a cautious tone. "But doesn't that imply Chad knew the poison was in the cookie?"

"Not necessarily," Johnny pointed out. "But we'll probably know more when we figure out a motive for the killing."

"You mean, whether Angela or Chad was the intended victim, yes?"

Johnny spoke slowly, pausing between sentences, as though he were thinking it through or waiting for her reaction. "I don't see the killer targeting an anonymous auction winner. As I said earlier, there was no way to know who would get your cookies, Rona."

"Yes, there *was* a way—" she said, but he started to argue. She raised her hand and stopped him. "No, wait, *listen*. Hear my theory. What if the killer planned to secure the winning bid on my donation and then planned to somehow doctor my cookies? It would be easy, Johnny. He could have paid off a stooge in the crowd to do his bidding. He'd avoid bringing suspicion on himself and money would be no factor if he wanted to kill. After winning, he could poison a few of the cookies and give them to his victim later as a gift. No one would even know he'd had a hand in it. After the intended victim ate a cookie or two and died, he'd be home free, and when the police discovered that some of the cookies contained poison, I'd be the prime suspect. Like I am. Horrible, but it would've worked."

"Would it have?" Johnny asked.

Rona frowned, rethinking the plot. "Why not? Everyone at the café would know that I'd made them."

Johnny held up his hand and stopped Rona's train of thought. "Except, it didn't get that far."

"Angela died before the sale even started."

"She had to have been poisoned before...or it was the cookie. Your cookie."

"No. It's horrible. But how?"

"Until we hear from Glenn, we're assuming the poison was in the cookies. Maybe it was in the tea she had at her house."

"Or my bakery item." She couldn't believe any of this.

Johnny kissed her hand. "Well, her visitor could have put the poison in the tea, out of the public eye. We're just assuming it was in the cookies because that's the last thing we saw her eat."

"Or it could have been in the cider she had at the café. We don't know."

He nodded and seemed to contemplate something. He ignored her last comment and frowned. Speaking slowly, he asked, "Do you know anything about Chad, anything personal, I mean? If we're to consider him an intended victim, as we've hinted at, because Angela offered him a cookie, and if that was the way the poison was administered, there has to be some motive for wanting him dead."

"I don't know him very well, Johnny. Sure, I frequent his café for lunch or dinner a few times a month, and he buys some of my bakery products for his menu offerings, but all I really know about him is that he likes to fish."

Johnny sighed heavily. "That doesn't quite do it. The days of fighting over fishing rights ended a while back, I think. Well, there has to be a reason for the murder. Or an opportunity to present the lethal food. As much as I hate to say it, my money's still on poison in the gingerbread drop."

"But how?" A strained silence fell between them as they considered various theories. Rona envisioned Angela's kitchen with two cups and plates in the sink, the table of cookies at the café with Angela grabbing one and eating it, and Glenn handing the platter to her.

"Debbie didn't get sick." Rona spoke so softly Johnny took several seconds to glance up.

"Sorry? What was that about Debbie?"

"Last evening. Debbie took one of my cookies at the beginning. She ate it while Angela was still doing the welcome spiel."

"I ate one on the drive over to the café and I'm fine. How did Debbie and I end up eating safe cookies? Luck?" Johnny's voice grew stronger. "So, if the cookies were tampered with, and if that was the delivery method of the poison, and if it was intentional, then that would mean the cookies would have had to be distinguishable."

"I don't know…that's a lot of 'ifs.' This scares me to death."

Exhaling deeply, Johnny tapped his fingers on the table. He spoke slowly, apparently thinking through what had taken place. "There had to be some visual marker, Ronnie. Debbie could've chosen any cookie from that platter, but she chose one with green frosting. Do you remember what cookie Angela took? Could you see?"

Rona nodded, remembering the event. "She held it up twice, when she asked Chad to eat a cookie and later when she sort of toasted the event. It was red and white."

"Are you sure?"

Rona snapped her fingers, smiling. "Positive. Debbie didn't hand it to Angela. Angela chose it from the tray, remember?"

"Now that you mention it, yes. She picked it up from the end of the tray, from the cookies nearest to her. It had white frosting looped over the red."

"Debbie must've added the white icing before Angela got it." She stood up, speaking more hurriedly in her enthusiasm. "Angela doesn't like the color green. She decorates with red and white for Christmas. She even wore red and white at the event. If the other cookies had red or green frosting, and one had red *and* white, Debbie was probably ninety-nine percent certain Angela would take the red and white iced one."

Johnny pushed his chair back as he got to his feet and wrapped his arms around Rona as though protecting her from what was to come. "We better tell Glenn so he can search her house."

Chapter Nine

Two hours later, Detective Glenn Somers, Rona, and Johnny stood in Debbie's kitchen. As Glenn explained it, he was there with a search warrant in connection with the death of Angela Hermitter.

"And you think I'm responsible?" Debbie stared at the man, her mouth slightly open, her eyebrows raised. "How do you propose I accomplished that?"

Glenn turned to Rona. "Would you like to tell her what you told me, or should I?"

Rona took a step forward. "I don't mind. Detective Somers told me the lab found larkspur seeds in the frosting drizzled on top of one of my cookies. He asked me who might've done that if I hadn't."

Debbie crossed her arms over her chest and sneered. "And your reply evidently was that I did. How convenient."

"I told him that on arriving at Chad's, I walked into the kitchen and Johnny handed the boxes of cookies to you. You took them, opened the top box, and began putting them on a platter."

"Congrats. That was my job that evening."

"You were the only person in that section of the kitchen at that time, Debbie. You could've added the white frosting to one with red icing."

"And why would I do that?"

"Because you wanted Angela to get the cookie with

the poison on it. You knew she didn't like the color green, and some of the cookies were iced with green. So you added the white, poisoned icing to one with red."

Debbie shook her head. "Amazing. And I suppose no one saw me whip up a batch of icing. No one was aware that I got out a mixing bowl and spoon, softened butter, added confectioner's sugar and milk and vanilla…" She stopped, her voice taking on a bitter edge. "You're desperate. You're trying to pin the murder *you* committed on anyone who was convenient. You're pathetic."

Rona continued, her voice calm as she explained. "It would be easy if you came prepared. You knew Angela would start the evening by eating a cookie because it's always done that way. And she'd eat one of mine since the custom is to eat a cookie made by last year's winning baker. You prepared the larkspur poison at home. You probably have seeds that you put into a batch of white icing. Maybe you put that in a pastry bag and concealed it in your pocket. Then when no one was watching, you doctored one or two cookies in the kitchen. That'd be easy to do and would take less than a minute."

"That's insane. You're grasping at straws."

"Could be," Glenn said, placing the warrant on the kitchen counter. "I'll tell you after I've looked around." Slipping on some plastic gloves, he nodded to Johnny. "Would you act as witness to my search, Mr. Murray?"

Johnny nodded, and they wandered into the living room. Glenn searched the area, then the two men gravitated to the hallway. "You want to watch me, Mr. Murray?" He opened the closet door and began looking through the coats in the closet. After several minutes, he took a coat out. "There's something of interest in this one." He brought it into the kitchen, draped it over the butcher-block island, and took a small metal tube from the garment's pocket. A plunger was screwed onto the top of the tube. Bits of white icing had seeped from the nozzle and flecks of icing smeared the pocket's interior. "I could be wrong. I've been wrong before. But I think the lab techs will find not only your fingerprints on this canister, but also the frosting laced with larkspur seeds. What do you think?" He held it up so Debbie could see it.

Her face had turned ashen, but her voice was strong. "I've never seen that before. One of you put it in there."

Glenn laid the decorating tool on the counter, then opened the cookbook lying next to the sink. The pages flipped open to reveal seeds in the book's gutter. Turning, he held the book toward Debbie. "And these just happen to be there by magic, I assume."

"You're absurd."

"Why would you have larkspur seeds—poisonous seeds of a poisonous plant—in a cookbook in the *kitchen*, of all places, unless you were cooking with it and cooking with an intent to kill?"

"I don't have larkspur plants. I ripped out my garden this past summer. My neighbor Mike can tell you. Besides, even if I had that plant, it doesn't bloom for another four months. Where am I supposed to have gotten the seeds for your fantastic plan?"

"Let's ask Mike if you got some seeds from him."

Debbie pressed her lips together.

Glenn approached her and said, "Put your hands behind your back."

Chapter Ten

Rona and Johnny sat on the couch in her back room, enjoying the heat from the fire crackling in the fireplace, while they sipped hot cider. Most of the snow had turned to slush by late afternoon, but once the sun set it began to refreeze, and somber shadows stretched toward the river. The woods had gone quiet, as though the night creatures listened from inside their dens and under leaves and in the trees. The air held the color and coolness of twilight, while letting in fingers of mist that crept through the dried remnants of the flowerbed and nestled at the base of the house. On the eastern horizon, the moon balanced on a treetop. The world seemed at peace, as though nothing could interrupt the ordinary flow of life.

"You want to come over for Christmas dinner, Johnny?"

"Won't the residents of Klim view an invitation to your ex-husband as a topic for their ill-lit alley chats?"

"The residents of Klim can't be more shocked than they already are. I've been linked to four foul deeds if your memory needs prodding. Besides, they won't wait to slink into an alley to gossip. Sunlit street corners or a churchyard are more to their liking." She linked her fingers through his and squeezed them as the fire popped. "You might want to come over. Santa told me he'll leave something for you beneath the tree."

"Thanks to Santa, but I hope it's not another tie. I

have a closetful of ties I never wear." He kissed her hand. "I've been wondering how I can utilize them in my art gallery. Use them instead of the more familiar beaded curtain?"

Rona shook her head and curled her legs under her. "Too gauche for your place."

"Well, I'll just pray Santa brings me something *else* I really want." He grinned and leaned over to kiss her but stopped when his cell phone rang.

He set his mug on the coffee table and yanked the phone from his pocket. After a minute, he logged off and tossed the phone onto a nearby upholstered chair. "That was Glenn."

"I gathered that. But the rest of your conversation needs translating. I didn't get much from 'Oh? Really? You're kidding.' A paragraph or two in English, using complete sentences, would be helpful."

"Debbie confessed."

"Jail has that effect on some people. I remember my dad telling me about his brother—"

"Do you want to hear this?"

Rona nodded and snuggled next to him. "I'm all ears."

"You're not. There are other things I like about you much more than your ears, but I won't bring that up now. Debbie confirmed your theory about piping on the white frosting, figuring Angela would take the doctored red-and-white cookie and eat it."

"Did she say why she did it?"

"She was interested in Chad."

"Chad! I never suspected that. Though I suppose I should have."

"Why? What makes you say that? Did she have a

photo of him in her house?"

"No, I wouldn't know about that, but when I was at Chad's, he said he didn't hear about Angela's death via Debbie—he added *'Thank God'* and referred to her as a leech. From the benefit of hindsight, I now assume that meant he'd had his fill of Debbie chasing him."

Johnny patted Rona's hand. "Mike dropped her, and then she tried to get Chad interested in her. That didn't work out either."

"At the auction, she tried to get him to take a cookie, but he pretty much ignored her." Rona recalled.

"She knew from Mike that Chad went over to Angela's house when Steve was out of town. I think Debbie figured if she killed Angela, Chad would gravitate to her. She seemed desperate."

"She must've been. An affair's not easy to break up," Rona said.

Johnny got up and put another log on the fire. "Which reminds me. The police finished their search of Angela's house."

"Why'd they do that? She wasn't killed there."

"Evidence, sweets. Those two cups and plates in the sink looked suspicious. They needed to look around to see if Steve had helped in the murder."

Rona patted the cushion beside her, and Johnny sat down. "Okay. Makes sense. What about Angela's house?"

"They found a dozen emails to her from Chad."

"Oh dear. Doesn't sound good."

"You're seeing the glass half empty, Rona. Glenn bent the rules and took a screen shot of the last email. Yes, I know, but it wasn't evidence in anything. It had nothing to do with Angela's murder. If you want to get technical, it's a private communication that has no right to be made public. But Glenn knew you and I wouldn't talk about it to anyone, and he thought you deserved to know the whole thing."

"Seeing as how I was the prime suspect, how thoughtful of him to smooth over the wound. What's in the email?"

Johnny brought up the message on his cell phone and handed it to Rona.

She read it as she leaned against his arm.

Angela—I sure hope you've kept everything from Steve. He's nearly impossible to fool. But it'll be worth all our secretive meetings when you tell him, and we see his expression. LOL! It took a while, but I did it. Got everything lined up for you. The week-long reservation at Sanibel Harbor Resort, the plane tickets, the scuba and sail boating lessons, the diving with the dolphins. He'll love it! Why wouldn't he? Going to football fantasy camp with the New England Patriots, talking to and playing with his idols... What a great idea you had. I'm just glad I could pull it off for you. I hope he appreciates you and all the time we put into this. He'll never forget this birthday!

When Rona finished reading the email, she collapsed against the back of the couch and pressed her fingers against her temples. "Oh, my lord. How horrible. Sort of puts a different slant on this, doesn't it?"

"There was no affair." Johnny's voice was soft, seemingly laced with sadness. He tucked a stray lock of her hair behind her ear and let his fingers trail down her cheek. "At least, not the suspected affair between Angela and Chad. Steve loved football, to the point where it put a strain on their marriage."

"Chad and Angela spent time together to plan this birthday gift. That's all they were doing." Rona slid her hand into his and squeezed it. He was more than her Lancelot. He was her anchor. "What a tragedy for everyone."

"It just reinforces what I've said all along, sweets. If you've found the love of your life, show her. Don't let her go."

Heat flood Rona's cheeks, and she glanced at him to see if he was serious.

His eyes stared back at her, dark and steady.

She glanced at the mantle clock. Its faint ticking filled the room as Johnny stared outside and the shadows danced on the far wall. "I wouldn't think of going anywhere. I'm staying put."

He stirred, smiling at her. "Good. I'm not busy the rest of my life, either. Except for January 28th. I'll be helping a buddy move. But the other 18,250 days are yours."

"How long is that?"

"Fifty years, give or take a leap day or two. I want to make sure I'm not skimping on our time together."

"You plan on living to be one hundred seven years old?"

"I don't see why not. I have to make up for our year of separation and divorce." He angled her head upwards and kissed her.

To Kat,
Best wishes,

Snow Kiss Cookies to Die For

by

Wendy Kendall

Wendy Kendall

Christmas Cookies Series

Dedication

To my sons Alex and Brad
Special thanks to Brad for his delicious, original and
sweet recipe for snow kiss cookies

Chapter 1

Recent events scared her. Desiree Tucker sat at her desk and struggled to get herself back on plan. She must finish the afternoon lessons for her first-grade classroom. Three years as a teacher at Bayside Elementary, proud of her students, her work, and a place where she got along well with all the staff, until now. Were they all out to get her for some reason? Ridiculous, but she couldn't ignore that someone was.

The tension in her own class sizzled between John and herself. Her other teaching assistants had been so easy to get along with. Then there was the substitute teacher next door, an epic nightmare. Why did Sara have to go on family leave this quarter? Simple tasks like maintenance requests to Kyle had become unbearable with his shady looks and resentful attitude. And then there was the whole different question of Leo. Oh yes, Leo. With a sigh she realized, she needed a vacation. Thank goodness winter break was just a week away.

The first graders squirmed in their seats and exchanged excited glances. Under their desks, legs were swinging. Impatience with math problems and overall restlessness was no surprise.

Today Desiree taught in a perfect storm of distractions. Friday afternoons always stir winds that lift flights of fancy about weekend fun to come. Add to that winter break just a week away. Then top it off with anticipation of a thunderous holiday treat announcement that teacher promised before they raced out the door. A look through the window revealed the icing on the day's delights. The rumored snow fluttered from the sky, raising hopes of a frosty weekend ahead. It seldom snowed in Bayside, and rarely more than a dusting, but whenever it did there was joy on young faces. Irresistible December magic. Desiree wanted to believe in magic again.

A high-pitched squeal grabbed Desiree's attention and her focus. Anna with her red-haired pigtails bouncing and Marlo with her long black curls dangling on her shoulders sat across from each other in the back corner. Their whispers abandoned when teacher had her eye on them. Suppressing a grin, Desiree shook her head and in a soft tone said, "Anna. Marlo." She pressed her finger against her lips.

Sitting in front of them, Sam stared at the snow. Not likely his workbook page was done. He already had his plaid winter jacket on, and he looked ready to run for the bus home. Desiree predicted he'd be an excellent sprinter one day. Across the room in the front row, Ronna and Ashley giggled together. They always followed directions, so their math problems were no doubt complete. Peter passed a wrapped bubble gum across the aisle to his buddy Jack. Before Desiree could react to either duo, the class door opened, and Leo walked in. The kids turned his way, breaking into broad and friendly smiles. He gave them a thumbs up and smiled back, then motioned for them to be quiet and behave, followed by his trademark mischievous grin.

Desiree lingered over Leo's easygoing manner and muscular build as she admired his sculpted physique in the long-sleeved t-shirt under his down vest. A lock of his black hair brushed across his forehead. She missed lovable, retired George Dalrow. Nice when he was replaced by a man in his twenties though, good looking, interesting, and fun.

He gazed at her as he approached. She was glad she'd chosen the cute red dress with the scoop neckline. A shiny black belt fastened at the waist and the skirt's flirty hemline stopped just above her knees. The matching pump shoes gave a little boost to her 5'4" frame. She hoped her blonde hair wasn't too messy after recess with the kids. She pushed it back over her shoulder. She was glad she'd applied a lipstick on her break.

He turned his back to the kids and leaned close to her. "Hi, Dez, always good to see you." He smiled and took a step back. "I came by to check on that radiator."

"Always nice to see you too."

"Well, let me get out of your way." Leo headed to do his work.

She watched him. He'd been such a friend since he'd joined the staff. They chatted most days. When he asked her out, she'd shook all over with excitement. What a night that was. Why didn't he ask her out again? Didn't he have a good time?

She checked her cell phone. Just ten minutes before the final bell and she needed to make her announcement. The adjoining door to the other first grade class opened. The substitute teacher stood in the doorway. She pulled her matching sweater set close over her slacks and looked in. One more distraction. Couldn't Madeline wait until after school if she needed something? Why wasn't she busy with her own class?

Dez stood and paced in front of her desk. "Pay attention, class. Close your workbooks and hand them forward." She nodded to her teaching assistant, John. He looked glum as always, like he was just here to fulfill his college requirements so he could graduate with a teaching degree. She'd enjoyed her own teaching assistant days. How happy she'd been working with kids and helping however she could. Was there something more she could do to inspire John?

Dez waited for all the workbooks to be collected before making her announcement. "We've been learning about different winter holidays and traditions. Next week we're going to play a winter game. It's called secret Santa."

The children leaned forward, eyes wide and mouths open. Peter raised his hand and asked, "How do we play? Is Santa coming here?" The other children started talking again.

Dez clapped her hands a couple of times. "Secret Santa is a game where you'll each make something nice for someone else in the class, without telling them it was you who did it. Every one of you will have a holiday stocking hanging on the wall in the room. Each day's homework will be a gift you'll make for that secret friend, and the gift will be put in their stocking. You'll also find a gift from your secret Santa in your stocking. On the last day of school before we go home for our winter break, we'll have a party and reveal who gave gifts to who. What do you think? Do you want to play?"

There were cheers and eager smiles. Leo laughed out loud. Some kids hopped out of their seats. John stood with his arms crossed over his chest, frowning. Madeline leaned against the door, tapping her fingers, and watching.

Ronna raised her hand. Dez pointed to her. "Quiet everyone. Yes, Ronna."

"Will there be treats at the party too? Will you bring those snow kiss cookies you told us about? Your favorites?"

"Treats for the party will be a surprise. On the counter at the back of the room are envelopes with each of your names. Inside is your first assignment, a holiday card to color. I've emailed your parents, so they know all about it. Monday morning I'll collect your cards and put them in the right stockings."

Conversations began again. Madeline had stepped back into the other classroom, leaving the door ajar. Dez motioned for quiet. "John, could you please walk the first row of students to the counter, and close the door at the back in case we get noisy."

John took the students to the envelopes. The others watched. Desiree stood in front of the next row. "Everyone else, get your jackets on so you're ready to go home."

Waves of activity rippled across the room. After everyone had their envelope, John lined the children up at the door. When Leo finished his work on the radiator, Dez delighted at how the line of children conveniently blocked his exit. Maybe she'd get a chance to chat with him.

Dez had the last of the students at the back counter as the bell blasted. She ushered them over to the line. "Enjoy your weekend everyone. Have fun coloring your cards and be sure to keep your secret until the party."

The children waved and said their goodbyes as John led them into the hallway and out to after school care, the buses, and parent pick up. Desiree waved back at the children, then stood and looked at Leo. "Happy Friday. How are you?"

Leo joined her. "Happy weekend. Those kids never have as much energy as when it's time to go home. They're sure excited about your secret Santa game. Sounds like a good idea, Dez."

Her pulse quickened as he stood next to her. She wished he stood a little closer. She really enjoyed his company. Maybe he'd ask her out this weekend. "I think the kids will have fun and learn too. I'm going to hang up the holiday stockings on the wall before I leave for the day."

Leo shook his head. "I won't hold you up. I'm happy to help with next week's holiday party, so you don't have to manage it all yourself. It'd be fun to do together. I mean, if you want to, Dez."

"I'd like that."

He stepped closer. "We should get together and talk about ideas then. If you're available tomorrow night, can I take you out to dinner? It would be fun to get started, and I'd like to take you out."

She felt a glow all over as her December wish came true. "That would be nice. Saturday night then."

He took her hand and held it for a moment. "I'll pick you up about 6:00." When he heard his name called from the doorway, Leo let go of her hand and stepped back.

Dez recognized the stilted voice immediately. Kyle, the other man from maintenance. He'd worked at the school longer than Dez. The opposite of Leo, taller, thinner, blond and his conversation left a lot to be desired. He was dull.

She waved, and he gave a quick wave back. "Hi, Desiree. Hey, Leo, sorry to interrupt. Water heater trouble again. I wanted to show you what I think is needed and get your sign off."

Leo put his hands on his hips. "Sure, yeah, I can come right now. We're done here. Just talking about what's needed for the holiday party. Thanks, Dez. See you soon."

Dez picked up the stack of students' workbooks. "Have a good weekend, both of you."

Kyle answered as he turned back to the hallway, "You too."

Leo gave her a grin and a wink. "I'll text you later," he said and disappeared out the door.

Chapter 2

The class windows overlooked the Bayside Elementary parking lot. Dez raised the blinds and looked at the transportation hub. A thin layer of snow laced the concrete, tempered by tire tracks from the idling buses and the lines of cars in the parent pick up lanes. Frosty footprints decorated the sidewalk, and exhaust from the vehicles fogged the scene. As buses chugged toward the road, vigilant school staff matched students to parents for their rides home. John steered his cluster of kids to the curb.

Happy daydreams of the weekend ahead, including her Saturday night date with Leo disappeared. Dez sat at her desk and prepared for the meeting she'd been dreading. John's progress review promised to be a difficult one. She wanted to help him, to encourage him, but his actions demonstrated he should pursue a career in another field. How would he react to her review, and conclusion?

While she waited for him to return, she took out the Santa stockings she'd bought for next week's festivities. They were the traditional red color with a white trim at the top, in a soft felt material. She'd print the students' names off her laptop to glue on each stocking, then decorate with a cardboard snowman. A delightful display.

She clicked on her cell phone and calculated the time before her coffee with Katherine Watson at Purse-onality Museum Cafe. The classroom door banged shut startling Dez.

John stood pigeon toed in his black sneakers in front of the first row of desks. His hands shoved deep in his jean pockets, his jacket hung down to his hips, and his cheeks were red from the cold parking lot. "Kids are all dropped off at after school care or headed home. You wanted to see me?" He looked at the stockings on her desk.

Desiree picked up the review folder. The coziness of the chairs in the reading circle might put them both at ease, or maybe just herself, or maybe not. The folder in her hand shook. "Let's sit here. I wanted to chat about your experience now that you've been in the classroom for several months."

John assumed his usual dejected look with his mouth in a tensed, thin straight line, downcast eyes, and sagging shoulders. He shuffled over and sat in the chair closest to the door.

Desiree sat down across from him and cleared her throat. "I'm working on your progress review for Principal Milner. On a positive note, you've been on time to work every day. When I give you specific tasks in the classroom, you complete them. You stick to the class schedule. You're reliable. Have you enjoyed working with the children?"

His eyebrows raised and his eyes widened as he looked directly at Desiree for the first time that day. She wondered why such a simple question would come as a surprise to him. She waited for his answer.

"Sure. Working with the kids is what I do."

Desiree looked down at her review paper. "Sometimes new teaching assistants can be unsure about how best to interact with the children." She looked up at him now, trying to land her message. "That's hard to learn in your college classes, it's different in person. What I've noticed...your enthusiasm...it's sometimes lacking. I'm suggesting you could be more personable with them. Try for meaningful interactions." Desiree stifled a sigh. She didn't want to patronize him. Was any of this sinking in?

John leaned back in his chair. "I've done everything you asked."

She plunged forward, "Let me give you an example. Part of your responsibility is to help them individually and in small groups as they learn new material. You haven't been involved with the kids that way. You haven't voiced much interest in lesson planning, which is a great way to understand what teaching is about, and whether you want to pursue that as your life's work."

In one sudden movement he stood up and glared at the folder in her hands. He spoke in a flood of words louder and louder. "Teaching's what I want, for sure. I come from a family of teachers. Just tell me what you want from me."

Desiree dropped the folder on the ground. She'd never seen emotion from John before. She left the papers on the floor, not wanting to look away from him, not sure what to do next. "If this is what you want to do, then let's calmly discuss it. Let's make a plan."

He sat and Desiree picked up the paper, giving her heart a chance to slow back to normal. She walked to her desk. "Let's get you in on lessons. Why don't you plan and teach Thursday's reading time circle? I'll be here to help with anything you need."

John frowned. "The whole lesson?"

Desiree jumped on the glimmer of enthusiasm. "Yes, first decide on the book, then how you'll present it, how the students will participate, and how you'll evaluate their comprehension."

John wrinkled his forehead and squinted. He stared at her. Desiree leaned against her desk and fought the impulse to take her tight shoes off, maybe throw one at him. It had been a long day. "Start by choosing the book you want to read from the shelves."

John agreed. "Okay. I'll do it."

Desiree debated whether to celebrate or call for reinforcements. "Let me know if you have questions." She pushed on, determined to make herself ask, "John, are you happy teaching here?"

He leaned back again in his chair. "Sure." He folded his arms across his chest. "The stockings have to be put up. The kids like that idea. Do you want me to hang them?"

Desiree said, "Let's do it together. You see this lesson is an opportunity for them to learn creativity and functional skills. They'll also learn the happiness that comes from giving. I can explain more as we create the display."

He remained motionless and stared at her. She wondered if it was a challenge. Desiree glanced away from his intensity. When she looked back, he smiled for the first time all day, at least the quick flash appeared smilish. "Sure."

The magic of the season strikes again, and maybe her talk helped too. "Great. I'll show you what needs to be done."

John shrugged his jacket off. A slip of paper fell out of a pocket and fluttered to the floor. A prescription? John stooped down, grabbed it, and stuffed it back in his jacket which he hung on the back of the chair. None of her business. She slipped the folder in her desk drawer. If she saw improvement next week, she'd update the review. If not, John's pre-holiday review would include little good cheer.

Chapter 3

Decorating the wall turned out to be the best collaboration Desiree had experienced with John. She was sorry when the connecting door to the other first grade class opened, and Madeline peeked in. "Glad, you're still here. Dez, can I borrow the smart whiteboard? I need it for Monday."

Desiree handed the last stocking to John while she composed herself and refrained from listing Madeline's many other needs. Why waste energy on frustration with Madeline's lack of planning, and coordination of shared equipment? Thank goodness Sara would be back to teach her class in January, and this annoying substitute would be history. "If you need it, go ahead. I had it reserved on the online equipment list, but I can rearrange my schedule."

"Thanks. I'll wheel it into my room."

John stepped back from the wall and looked out the window. Dez followed his gaze but didn't see anything special. John went for his jacket. "If we're done, I need to get going."

Desiree said, "Yes, all done. Have a good weekend. Next week will be busy."

John rushed out the door.

"Desiree, if you have a minute, I wanted to talk to you."

Desiree startled at hearing Madeline's voice. Hadn't the woman left? "Yes, fine. What about?"

Madeline walked over and stood beside Dez. As she spoke, she leaned in even closer. "It's about my future. With Sara back after the break, I'm without a job. I'm a good teacher, and I like this district. I'm applying for another position. I have references, but I want to be sure I don't have anyone saying things against me. I want to be sure you don't."

Desiree knew exactly what Madeline was talking about. She stepped back to gain personal space from Madeline's crowding stance, but her back bumped against the counter. Madeline left no room to ease away from her. Dez faced her squarely. "I can't unsee something you did this morning."

Madeline's hot breath scented with onions no doubt leftover from lunch seared the inches between them. "You can forget it, not mention it, leave me alone. Don't start trouble. I wasn't stealing that money. I put it back. You saw it wrong."

Desiree shook her head. "If someone asks me, I can't lie. Please move away."

She brushed against Madeline's shoulder to walk past her, but the woman stood her ground. "Look, I need a job. I've tried to be nice, but you've never liked me. I'm telling you, leave me alone and keep your mouth shut or you'll be very sorry."

She was shaking, but this time Desiree pushed through and walked over to her desk. She picked up her cell phone. "Don't threaten me. I saw you steal money out of the office cash drawer. I'm obligated to report it."

Madeline stuck her chin out and pouted. "It's your word against mine. Don't forget that." She walked over to the whiteboard and wheeled it to the connecting door. She looked over her shoulder. "I was trying to be nice about this. You're the mean one. You started it." She gave one last, lingering, stormy look and slammed the door shut.

Dez sat down and slowed her breathing as she realized how nervous she'd become. She wished that connecting door had a lock.

Chapter 4

Snow flurries tickled her cheeks. Her unbuttoned coat flapped as she walked to her old, second hand, blue, beloved sports car. It was one of four vehicles left in the lot. Her tote bag had papers to work on at home. She put it in the trunk, safely stowed for her visit with Katherine. She closed the trunk and a movement by the playground gate caught her eye. Kyle and John stood talking.

Dez unlocked her car door and got in. Kyle put his hands on his hips, and John waved his arms as he talked. She put her glasses on, ready to drive. Now she could see them more clearly. John handed Kyle something. Money? A paper? Kyle glanced at it before taking a small bag out of his jacket pocket and giving it to John. She'd seen enough. She turned the key and the engine roared to life, blasting the serenity of the soft wintry scene. She cringed when the men turned to look. John's gaze zeroed in on her.

She put the car in gear and lurched forward. She stepped on the brake before jumping the curb. John and Kyle watched. She looked down so there was no mistake again. With the car in reverse, she backed out of the spot and steered away and out the exit. She never glanced back, not even in the mirror, as she drove onto the street.

More complications with John. Great. Whatever he was doing didn't look like it belonged on school property. Desiree knew it would be her responsibility to talk to him. After the strange day she'd had, she was very happy the weekend lay ahead. Saturday night with Leo too.

A loud, sustained car horn drowned out even her noisy car engine. She swerved back onto the right side of the yellow line. A pickup truck whizzed by in the opposite direction. The driver waved his fist at her. She reached the stop sign at the end of the block. She sat there letting her nerves calm and her head clear. Daydreaming can be deadly.

The car behind her flashed its lights, brightening the reflection in her mirror. She looked both ways again and crossed the intersection. Bayside was bustling. What a relief to arrive at Katherine's museum. Her cell phone beeped. She got it out of her purse and saw a new text. No sender showing. She hesitated, then opened it. After reading, she was stunned.

You have a choice to make. Choose wisely. Don't make a fatal mistake. I'm watching you. Either way, we'll be together.

She read the short message again. Her stomach tightened. What was it about the words? You have a choice to make...the same thing Fred had said when she told him she was leaving him. Was he tormenting her too? She shuddered as she shut the screen off and put the phone away.

A festive Main Street adorned her windshield view. Holiday decorations in the snowfall delighted shoppers and children as they dashed around the stores. She looked for any of her students, but everyone was too bundled to recognize from a distance. Sandy's bakery, with its ever present sweet baked bread scent, had drawn a crowd. A couple of blocks down from there was the roundabout. It had been transformed with the tall community Christmas tree.

She got out of the car and heard soft jingling. She scanned the scene. By the theater on the corner a jolly looking man shook a stick of bells, and a family donated to his kettle. She took a deep breath of the pine air and soaked in the joy around her. She chuckled as she noticed the line of children at the entrance to the little candy cane lane near the toy store. They hopped from foot to foot with excitement for their turn to see Santa.

Energized by the enchanting downtown, Dez walked across the sidewalk and past the open picket gate, through the yard and up the front steps. On the porch the sign said 'Open' and 'Welcome to the Museum'. She walked in and entered the heat of the tropics. There was Katherine in the hallway fiddling with the thermostat on the wall. She was bundled in a lavender turtleneck encased in a long, thick, grey sweater and jeans.

Dez wiped her shoes on the door mat. Katherine wore sleek, grain leather boots with cream colored fur trimming the top, just under the knees. "Katherine, hi. I finally made it. Hot enough in here for you?" She always enjoyed teasing Katherine.

"I'm so glad you're here. Time for a hot latte and a break. And no, it's not hot enough in here for me. Not yet."

"I miss the Montana snowstorms, and you miss the Southern California heat."

"I sure do."

Dez loved how their friendship just seemed to click, despite their differences. She hung up her coat on the rack and followed Katherine on a quick pass through the 1920's and 1930's exhibits, toward the open doors of the cafe. As she glanced at the showcases of vintage purses and historic photos with captions and posted narratives, Dez got excited for the January field trip she'd reserved for her class to hear history stories and see the collection. On her right was a wonderful display of purses the Suffragettes carried. Next to that a description of shipboard travel and samples of luggage. She made a mental note to follow up next week with a couple of permission slips that had not yet been returned. No sense waiting until the last minute.

The touch on her arm interrupted her mental to-do list. "Sorry, it's been a crazy day. What did you say?"

Katherine laughed and steered her toward a stool at the counter. "You need a drink. How about a new peppermint latte recipe I created for the holidays?"

Desiree sat and leaned back. "Yes, please. It's quiet in here today. Where is everybody? This place is usually so busy."

Katherine finished washing her hands and began creating the drinks. "Oh, it was very busy earlier. You're here fashionably late, and it's almost closing. It's perfect. We can have a nice chat and get all caught up. So why was your day crazy?"

Desiree hung her purse on one of the hooks under the bar. "Busy, busy, busy, but I have some super news. You'll never guess it."

Katherine wiped her hands with a bar towel, tilted her head to the side, and gazed at the ceiling. "Wait. Let me think."

Desiree grinned. "You're wasting your time. Never in a million years, you won't get it."

Katherine waved a hand at her. "I know. You've saved up enough money for a new car. You need one. That old car of yours is not reliable."

Desiree shook her head. "No not a car. Leo asked me out tomorrow night."

Katherine handed her a latte and held up one of her own. "Cheers to that. A second date. That's good news."

Desiree sipped her latte, then set it on the counter and clapped her hands. "We had such a great time on our first date, and it's taken him awhile to ask me out again. I always enjoy talking with him at school. He's taking me to dinner. I have to figure out what to wear."

Katherine said, "Stop by tomorrow afternoon when you know what you're wearing, and you can borrow a purse."

Desiree laughed. "Thanks for the offer, but I don't think I'll have time."

Katherine leaned forward against the counter and wrapped her fingers around the warm cup. "There's nothing like a new man to take your mind off an ex."

Remembering that Fred may have been the one who sent her that sick text made Desiree choke on her peppermint drink. She coughed and gasped. Katherine asked if she was okay, and all she could do was shake her head. Next thing she knew a glass of water was in her hand, and she opened her eyes to see Katherine's concerned look. She sipped the water and regained her breath.

Katherine sat on a stool next to her. "Did I say something wrong?"

The wave of fear pulsed through her again. "Leo asking me out was the best part of the day. The rest was weird. I got this scary text. It doesn't show who the sender is. I almost deleted it thinking it was spam, but then I looked at it again. It's awful. I think it was written by Fred."

Katherine watched her. "No. Not your ex."

Dez grabbed her cell. "It kind of freaked me out. Listen."

She clicked onto the screen. "It starts out: You have a choice to make. Choose wisely. Don't make a fatal mistake. I'm watching you. Either way, we'll be together."

The frown on Katherine's face didn't make Dez feel any better. Dez's eyes teared. "A choice to make. That's what he said to me when I left. Is Fred trying to tell me he wasn't cheating with that girl? He'll never convince me of that. It's over between us. Why does he keep on? I see his car drive past my apartment sometimes. Is that why it says he's watching me? It gives me the creeps. Remember those flowers I got? No card? I gave them to the Senior Center. He calls me and I just don't answer. He's texted me too, but never on a blank number. Why would he do this?"

Katherine said, "Whoever it is, I don't like the tone of it, the word fatal, or that it's anonymous."

Dez clicked off her phone screen and put it away. "Why would anyone send this message to me? I'm sure it's Fred. He better stop."

Katherine shook her head. "You might have to get a restraining order. Maybe the police can trace the text. I could check with Jason."

"Let me think about it. Let's see if I get any more." Desiree finished her drink. "This latte tastes so good. It really was a rough day. Besides this text, I also had to talk with John about his work. It was uncomfortable, but we had a breakthrough. We worked together on a lesson for Monday."

"That's good then."

"Until I walked out to my car and saw him dealing drugs or something suspicious right at the school. Now I'll have to deal with that. Oh, Katherine please don't say anything. I shouldn't have said that. I really don't know the facts yet."

Katherine took both cups to the sink. "Don't worry, I won't say a word to anyone. I hope he's not involved in anything illegal. The few times I've seen him he always looks sad, like he has a lot going on. He keeps to himself."

Dez leaned forward and propped her chin on her hand. "You know I don't usually talk about people like that. I think I'm still worked up inside about a fight with Madeline. You know, she's the substitute teacher I mentioned to you."

Katherine came back to the counter. "A fight?"

Dez stared back at her. "She's mad because I caught her stealing money from the office fund drawer this morning. She had the nerve to deny it, call me names, cause a scene. She was very intimidating. The office was closed by the time I got out of there, but I'm reporting her to the principal next week."

Katherine gave her a hug. "You poor thing. You really did have a day. Maybe we should have been drinking something stronger after all."

Dez shook her cares away. "It's okay. The day is done, and I have Saturday night with an amazing guy to look forward to."

Katherine sat down. "Leo is cute."

Dez warmed to the new topic. "He's not just cute. He's nice and smart, with such a great sense of humor. At school we see each other and talk. Our first date was so romantic. We had dinner at the amazing Toreador restaurant. We sat close and lingered almost four hours. Can you believe it? We closed the place down. Then we walked along the beach and he had his arm around me. It was cold. The wind was blowing. He suggested we ride the ferry. I didn't want the night to end. We sat inside the ferry, holding hands, staring out at the beautiful, starry night with a full moon. He drove me home, then he kissed me. What a kiss. And now we're going out tomorrow night." Dez clapped her hands together.

Katherine said, "No wonder you're looking forward to going out again."

Dez hesitated, but she couldn't hold it in. She had to tell someone and here was her trusted friend. "He's different, Katherine. I think he's the one for me. I feel it. I've never felt this way before. I waited and hoped he'd ask me out again. I almost asked him, but I decided I needed to hear the words from Leo. I couldn't bear for this to be like with Fred, where I'm not his one and only. I wanted to hear Leo say that he wants to go out, with me."

Katherine said, "And he did. Don't go overboard. It's just a second date. Get to know more about him."

Dez didn't know if it was the caffeine in the latte or her excitement, but she needed to move. She needed to work off some of this new energy. "I'm going to leave you to your Friday night. It's been so good to see you."

She stood up and hugged Katherine. "I'm glad you came by. Everything will work itself out. Enjoy your weekend. But Dez, let me know if you get any more of those texts. I'd be happy to ask Jason to investigate them for you, for a police perspective."

The ladies walked together to the front door. Dez grabbed her coat and gave Katherine another hug after buttoning up. Katherine closed the door quickly after saying goodbye, and Dez chuckled over poor Katherine shutting out the Bayside winter. She looked up and let the snowflakes dance on her face while she celebrated the sweet anticipation of her romantic weekend ahead.

Chapter 5

Dez slept in Saturday morning. The rest of the day was a December whirlwind of activity. With her date less than an hour away, visions of sweet romance danced in her head.

She put the dress on, adjusted the off-the-shoulder straps to just the right angle and looked in her full-length mirror for an overall appraisal. Yes, the black, form fitting dress with the sparkling bodice, and close at the waist, flowing over her hips, and down in a tight skirt to just above her knees was sure to be a hit. She twirled around to see the back and the dainty rose tattoo that showed, then she faced the mirror again. It was her favorite dress. A not-so-cheap copy of a real designer dress and very flattering.

The black tinged nylons completed the look, along with the gleam in her eye. She laughed and grabbed her hairbrush to attack her blonde curls that bounced on top of her bare shoulders. She went in the bathroom to finish her makeup. Leo had called and suggested she dress up for their night out, but he wouldn't give any hints about where they were going. He said it was a Christmas surprise. She took out her expensive jasmine perfume and applied it, not too much but enough to notice. She paused and imagined Leo's arms around her, pulling her close to him. She grabbed her three-inch spike heeled black shoes out of the closet and took one last look in the mirror. He'd never seen her like this, her own Christmas surprise. In the living room she sat on the couch to put on her heels and switch to her glittery evening clutch.

At the doorbell chime she hopped up and answered with a coy smile that grew into complete delight. Leo's deep brown eyes mesmerized. His black hair was slicked back. His shoulders somehow looked even broader in the tuxedo he wore.

His deep voice drew her look back up to his eyes. "Dez, you're beautiful. The night awaits dear lady, but first a sweet start in honor of your secret Santa game."

He dangled a miniature Christmas stocking in front of her. She took it, looked inside, and saw delectable, gaily wrapped candies. "Leo, how nice. Thank you." She gave him a hug. He held her to him a few seconds longer than friends, and she liked that. "Let me just grab my coat."

He stepped inside and helped her put the coat on. "It's a shame to cover up this gorgeous dress." He gently pulled her hair out from under the collar and whispered in her ear, "This is a special night." She turned around, and he took her hand. She blushed at the warm touch, and how his fingers interlaced with hers. "Let the adventure begin. After all, I have to get the suit back by midnight." He laughed and led her out the door.

She was surprised when he turned his compact hatchback car away from Bayside and headed south toward Seattle. He turned off the freeway before the city and meandered down to the docks at the lake. Lined up under the bridge and along the canal dozens of boats and houseboats were moored. Leo parked the car in a lot by a trail to the boats.

He put his hand over hers. "Just a minute."

He raced around the car to open her door and took hold of her hand again as they walked on the trail. The boats glittered with Christmas lights on the masts and hulls, some even had decorated trees prominent on their decks. A fishing boat quietly motored under the bridge, leaving just the slightest wake that lapped against the boats.

"Leo, this is beautiful." She stopped walking and tugged on his hand. "I'm not dressed for a hike though. These shoes won't travel well."

Leo put an arm around her shoulder. "Don't worry, no hiking tonight. We're just going over here, to the Moorish Delights." He pointed to the boat just ahead. Its name was lit in Christmas lights that also circled the deck. He jumped on board and then held out his arms to help her. Dez grinned. She took off her shoes and held them by the back straps as she stepped across onto the boat. He steadied her, and she regained her balance in the rocking vessel.

"Welcome to my home sweet home."

Dez looked around. "I didn't know you live on a boat."

Leo gazed across the deck. "I inherited it from my dad. I don't talk about it much. It's old and I'm fixing it up. It's my refuge, I guess. The city is close, but it feels far away."

Dez slowly twirled around, taking it all in. The air was cold, but the moon was bright and reflected on the water along with the lights. Stars were out, and the sound of the lapping water against the docks was calm. She faced Leo. "Am I dreaming?"

He watched her with a wistful look. They turned to gaze at the lake. He stood behind her with his arms wrapped around her shoulders. They spoke in whispers of dreams and hopes and wishes and laughed together over silly stories and funny anecdotes. Dez hadn't realized the sincere dedication and life purpose they both shared for the happiness and education of children. She was delighted to hear of the volunteer tutoring Leo did with children too, and they dreamed someday of opening a school together. Dez drank in the velvet of the night and the nearness of him.

Leo turned her to him. "I have a surprise below deck. Let me show you."

Dez walked with him. He opened a door, and they went down the stairs into a seating area that wrapped around a table. It was set for two with a mismatched array of plates, silverware, and wine glasses. In the center two candles waiting to be lit stood within a heart shaped holly wreath.

"Oh, Leo."

He walked to the table and lit the candles. "If you would like to be seated, dinner will be served." He took her coat and hung it on a hook before moving to the kitchen.

She savored the view of the water through the small window. As she looked back the way they'd come in, she could see a bedroom to the right of the stairs. In the galley, as Leo called it, he stirred the crock pot. He was chatting about the beef bourguignon, and that he'd pour the wine in just a minute. Dez dropped her shoes on the floor next to her, sat back and relaxed.

It was a delicious dinner, and Dez was thrilled afterwards when Leo proposed taking the boat out on the lake. She reached to slip on one of her shoes. Leo knelt on one knee in front of her, picked up the other shoe and slipped it on her foot. He touched the red heart tattoo on her ankle, looked up with a mischievous smile and winked.

After he helped her with her coat, they walked up on the deck and she watched him untie from the dock. Then Leo took the wheel. Dez stood next to him and they puttered away from the dock and through the canal, out into Lake Union. When they were far out in the middle, Leo cut the engine and let the boat drift with the soft sway of the currents.

They stared at the distant lights along the shore, and love touched their cheeks in the faint breeze that swirled around them. Leo slid his fingers under her chin. He tilted her face up, drew even closer and kissed her with a passion that warmed her even on this December night. Dez immersed herself in his affection.

When they came up for air they hugged, and he held her close. "Dez, I've never felt like this with anyone. You've touched a part of me no one has. I want to hold you forever, share adventures together. How does someone fall in love so fast? It's impossible, but I feel like I've loved you since that first day we met. You wore that cute blue dress with the polka dots, and you stopped me in the hall to let me know about a burned-out light in your classroom."

Dez looked up at him. "I have a confession. After I left you that day I went to the room and loosened one of the working bulbs so you wouldn't know I just made up that excuse to talk with you."

Leo grinned. Then he laughed, and Dez joined in. "You really saw me."

Dez said, "I have another confession. I think I love you too." He lifted her off her feet and twirled her around in the moonlight. They danced slowly to imaginary music and kissed again. They spoke of love in soft whispers. In time Leo slowly shook his head. "I'm going to be sorry in the morning that I said this, but I should probably get us back to dock."

When they got back Dez held the wheel while he tied up the boat. They cleaned up the galley. He handed her the holly wreath heart centerpiece. "For you. Shall we go?"

He helped her off the boat and used a flashlight as they walked up to the car. They chatted nonstop all the way back to Bayside about so many topics that interested them both. On Main Street the last movie at the theater was just letting out. Leo slowed and stopped at the intersection to let some of the people cross. "I'm not ready for this night to end." He looked at Dez, and then past her through the window.

She agreed. "Me too."

He grinned at her and switched on his turn signal. He steered the car around the corner toward the ferry dock. He parked outside the windowed entrance to the cafe. "How about an ice cream dessert? Ginardo's isn't closed yet."

She unbuckled her seat belt. "Ice cream in winter. Fun idea. I'll race you to the door." She grabbed her purse and then laughed as Leo rushed out of the car. The wreath was tangled in the string strap of her clutch, so she just grabbed both. Her high heels were a distinct disadvantage in the race.

She hurried to the cafe where Leo stood smiling. He took her in his arms with a big kiss. When he let her go, the curtain rustled in the window. The little bell jingled as he ushered her in. She greeted the cafe owner, "Hello Mr. Ginardo. We're so glad you're still open."

"Ciao. We're getting ready to close but there's still time. Leo, come va, how are you? It's been too long since I've seen you."

"Hey Arturo. How are you, and the family?" Leo stepped forward and his friend came around from the counter and slapped Leo on the back as they spoke together. Dez looked out the window at the beach and the ferry crossing. There were three women at a table finishing up dishes of ice cream. As they stood, she recognized Madeline.

Dez nodded and turned toward the counter. As Madeline passed, she took a full look up and down the length of Dez who became self-conscious about her heels and dress. She buttoned up her coat.

Madeline said, "Interesting to see the company you keep." Then she walked out with her friends. Dez wrinkled her nose thinking how rude that woman always was. She looked at Leo, but he had his back to her. She shook off the sudden chill in her mood and walked over to the men, mustering back her enthusiasm for the romantic night.

Leo put his arm around her waist. "Arturo is recommending his tartufo. What do you think?"

He dangled a tiny spoon in front of her and she tasted a most exquisite mixture of chocolate, hazelnut, and cherry. Her eyes grew wide and she smiled. Leo laughed and turned to Arturo. "I think we have a winner."

Back in the car they shared a dish of the ice cream as they watched the moonlit bay and the ferry boats. The light in Ginardo's went out and the owner drove home.

Leo said, "Do I have to take you home? I could stay like this forever."

She snuggled against his shoulder. "Me too."

He rubbed his hand slowly up and down her arm. "I hope we'll have many nights together."

They kissed, and lingered, then he started the engine and drove her home. He parked across the street from her building and kissed her good night. She got her keys out and reached for her heart wreath. He opened his door and she brushed against his arm. "Thank you for a wonderful evening. Don't bother getting out. I'm just going to run across the street and right into my apartment. No problem. I can't wait to see you again."

She gave him a quick kiss and got out. He stood up next to his car. She blew him another kiss as she crossed. She was conscious of him watching her. She looked back, and Leo had started after her. Nearby she heard an engine, then a car picked up speed. She looked to her right and saw a black sedan with its headlights off speeding at her. She ran to the curb and up on the grass. She turned back to see Leo running out of the way. He dove over the curb and rolled onto the grass too. The car screeched tires as it skidded around the corner and out of sight.

Leo got up and took her hand. "Are you okay?"

"I think so. I didn't even see him until... Are you okay?"

He brushed off his tux. "I just hope there's no rips or grass stains on the rental." He looked up at her and grinned. "I'll walk you up to your place."

He stooped to pick up the heart wreath she'd dropped and handed it to her. "Crazy nut. Wish I'd got his license plate. Probably drinking."

Dez wasn't sure. Had it been intentional? Was someone after her? There was one person she knew had a black sedan.

Chapter 6

On Sunday Dez luxuriated in reflections of the night before. She tenderly placed the heart wreath on her kitchen table as a centerpiece.

She texted Katherine, *What a night. Do you believe in Christmas miracles and true love? I do now.*

When her cell beeped later, it was a response from Katherine and thankfully not the anonymous sender.

Sounds like a good time. Can't wait to hear all about it.

Dez took Katherine literally and called her right away to fill her in.

On the drive to work Monday morning, Dez noticed all black sedans. There'd been no threatening texts since Friday. In fact, other than Katherine's text, the only others had been the most romantic treasures from Leo. She'd relished and responded to those.

She drove into the parking lot and focused on her morning ahead. Her students would be excited before the break, plus the tantalizing secret Santa fun would need to be managed. She walked down the hallway conscious of the click of her pumps on the linoleum and the swish of her tan khaki pants. Her colorful winter sweater offset the bland slacks.

Dez hoped to run into Leo first thing, to say good morning. It was just as well she hadn't since she was late. She opened her class door and got right to work setting up for the day. The shared door with Madeline's room stood ajar. On the wall, there was an extra stocking. It had glitter all over it, sparkling stars, and her name Dez. She took it off the hook. There was something inside. John swung the adjoining door wide open and walked in carrying a box.

Madeline followed. "Oh wait, here's one more." She slipped a smaller box on top of what he was carrying. She looked at Desiree. "Good morning. John, let me know if I can help with anything else. Glad I was in early for you."

John said good morning to Dez. "I'm getting ready for the reading group lesson for Thursday." He thanked Madeline and walked over to his desk.

Voices and laughter echoed as students came in from the hallway. Peter and Jack rushed up to Dez and said together, "Cool stocking."

She put the stocking back on its hook. "Good morning. Please put your secret Santa cards on my desk, and then take your seats."

Madeline said, "An admirer? Is that really appropriate at school?" She walked through to her room, closing the door behind her.

Dez reminded herself to get with Principal Milner today about how she'd caught Madeline. She considered what Madeline had said. An admirer? Maybe the stocking was from Leo. How nice of him. How fun.

It was a very busy morning. Dez was happy that John's mood had improved, and he was trying to engage with the kids. She'd still have to ask him about his actions on the schoolyard Friday. She shuddered remembering that stare he'd given her across the parking lot.

He took the class out for recess. Dez made a beeline for her stocking. Her excitement matched her students' as she took down her stocking and reached inside. She pulled out the cardboard, and her heartbeat sped up. One look and her heartbeat pounded.

The card was a picture of Santa in his sleigh with reindeer. Her smile faded seeing a cut out photo of her face pasted on the drawn figure next to Santa. Where did that picture come from? The caption read: *Secret Santa may sleigh you if you're not a good girl*

No signature. A secret and creepy Santa. Would Leo give her this? There was a bump in the toe of the stocking. She shook it upside down over the counter and a sprig of holly with berries fell out. From Saturday night's heart wreath?

Dez looked around, including out the windows. Was anyone watching? The idea of someone putting up a stocking with her name was odd enough, but with this inside? She rushed across the room and stuffed it all in her desk drawer. She texted Katherine to please set up time for her to talk with Jason after school.

She put down her phone and prepared the children's cards for the stockings. She was absorbed in her work when her phone vibrated. Relieved to hear back from Katherine so soon, she looked. It was from the anonymous sender.

Her hand shook as she clicked on it and read. *How did you like your card?*

Chapter 7

Leo enjoyed the spring in his step at Bayside Elementary early Monday morning. He hadn't seen Dez's car in the lot, but he'd turned down the hallway of her classroom just in case she was there. He wanted to say good morning. Maybe she'd want to go out after work.

He looked through the window in the door but saw only John and Madeline in Dez's classroom. They stood talking at the back of the room next to the stockings display. He smiled thinking how excited Dez would be with the secret Santa surprises. Madeline noticed him and waved. Leo nodded and gave a friendly wave back but decided not to go in. He needed to start work anyway. He'd see Dez later.

In the maintenance office Kyle sat on the edge of the desk looking at the computer screen, his back to the door. Unusual for him to be on the computer. "Hey Kyle. How was your weekend?"

The image on the screen disappeared and the district email popped up. "Hey Leo. Yeah it was good, too short. What about you? How did your Saturday night go?" Kyle straightened up and looked at him.

"Oh y'know, it was good. We had a great time. Glad it didn't rain."

Kyle turned back to the screen "I asked her out once. It didn't happen. Are you taking her out again?"

Surprised at the questions, he decided this was his own fault for confiding in Kyle last week before he asked Dez out. He stepped forward and pointed at the screen. "Oh yeah, planning on it. Are these today's priorities from the office? I can start with the top one."

Kyle gave a thumbs up. "Sounds good."

On his way to the door, Leo grabbed the extended reach tree pruner. "After that snow, I'm going to check the fir trees around the playground for any problem branches."

Kyle clicked the screen off. "There wasn't that much snow."

Leo started out the door. "Doesn't hurt to check, just in case. See ya later."

The Monday number one task was the priority. By the time he'd finished with that the kids were out at morning recess. Concerned about branches that might be a danger, Leo headed straight out to the playground ready to prune. Before he could get to the fence line, he was surprised by Madeline's voice calling him.

"Hi, what's up?"

She walked to him. "I'm with the kids for their recess and just wanted to say hello."

Leo scanned the grounds. "Is your assistant out sick today?"

She pointed toward the swings area. "Rachel's here. The kids are so excited with the holidays I decided to help keep an eye out in case she or John need help. I'm very conscientious. By the way, Desiree couldn't wait to tell me all about your date Saturday."

Uncomfortable, Leo didn't know what to say. "Oh? She talked to you about it?"

Madeline glanced around and stepped closer. She lowered her voice. "Maybe you had a good time. I just don't want you to get hurt. You're a nice guy. Be careful. I mean, she was laughing about your car. She joked about what she called a stupid heart wreath. She rolled her eyes about ice cream dessert. I told her I didn't want to hear any more, I mean because it's not right since we work together."

Leo was confused. What she said didn't sound like Dez at all. "She told you she didn't have a good time?"

Madeline paused and looked in his eyes, then shook her head. "Oh no, she's having a good time laughing about it. She wants to add you to her list of guys."

Leo took a step back. "That doesn't sound like Dez. Thanks for your concern, but I'm fine."

Madeline watched him. He didn't want to be rude, so he pretended to be adjusting the pruners. "I need to get back to work."

She said, "Me too. I'm just saying, be cautious. I'm caught in the middle here, friends with both of you. I mean, her last relationship ended because of cheating. I hope that won't happen with you."

Leo headed out along the fencing to check the tree branches.

Chapter 8

Dez turned her cell phone off. Her hand shook as she secured it in her desk. John brought the students back from recess, and she focused on her job. During lunch she attempted to meet with the principal about Madeline. No luck, he had a busy schedule today too.

Dez walked back to her room. Leo came to mind. It would be nice to bump into him now. It would be nice to see him sometime today, or at least hear from him. Or had she heard from him already? Was that stocking from him? The text? She needed to talk to Jason.

After last recess it was stocking time. Standing by the display, Dez addressed her students who listened with eager expressions. "Homework for tomorrow's secret Santa gift—you'll each take home an envelope with everything to make one ornament, and you can color it however you want. Any questions?"

Everyone fidgeted. "John is going to call you back one row at a time. He'll help each of you see what's inside your stocking."

She put a homework envelope on each desk and sat down at the front of the room. Just a few minutes left. She could keep her composure. The kids would be busy for the last minutes before going home. She hoped she'd see Jason. She forced herself to turn on her cell phone while keeping an eye on activity in the room. A text back from Katherine, and that was the only new one. Good.

Jason will be there when school ends. If he's late, stay in your class and wait. Let me know if I can do anything. Stop by later and we can talk.

Kids were giggling and showing each other their cards. How great it is to have friends. This was the first time since she'd looked in the stocking that Dez felt like she wasn't alone. Jason would help her. The bell rang and school was over. She busied herself with the normal routine, lining the kids up for John to take out to after school care, buses, and parent pick up. After the kids happily marched out with their envelopes, Dez lingered in the doorway. No sign of Jason.

She tackled the papers on her desk, putting some in her tote bag to work on that night. She paced the rows of desks, picking up dropped crayons, books or papers and putting them away. She ended up at the back of the room by the supply cabinet. She checked for stickers and printer paper.

Madeline opened the door to the other class. "I'm done with the whiteboard. Do you want it back against the wall?"

"Yes, thanks."

Madeline rolled it over and secured it. She walked back, then stopped and fingered the doorknob. "Thank you for not reporting what you thought you saw. Thanks for giving me a second chance. I guess I was wrong about you."

Dez crossed her arms. "You weren't wrong. I couldn't get in to see Mr. Milner today. I'll report it to him as soon as I can. It's my responsibility."

Madeline glared at her. She took two steps toward Dez, but John walked in from the hallway. Madeline turned and slammed the door behind her.

149

John grabbed the book on his desk. "I can't stay late today, but I'm taking the book for Thursday's reading lesson home. I'll work on it tonight. I'll have something for you to look over tomorrow. Is that okay?"

"Yes, that's fine. I just need to talk with you about something before you go."

He edged closer to the door and looked at the window, then again at Dez. "Sure. What is it?"

Dez smiled. "You did some good work today. I noticed you were more engaged with the students, and more upbeat, more confident. I wanted you to know I noticed the improvement, and I'm looking forward to seeing your lesson plan."

John put the book under his arm and his hands in his jacket pockets. "Thanks. Today was a good day." He walked to the door.

Dez cleared her throat. "Wait." After John gave her his full attention she continued, "After work on Friday I saw you at the playground gate with someone. I'm not sure what I saw but...if you're doing something inappropriate, at least you need to make sure you're not on school property."

John took a few steps toward her and swung a hand forward. "I was with Kyle. It was all school business."

The knock on the hall door startled her. Dez saw the police uniform through the window. Jason walked in. "Am I interrupting anything?"

"Jason, thanks for coming."

John looked to see who it was. When he turned back, he gave Dez a long, hard stare that started ice forming in her veins. She stammered, "John, we're done for today."

He straightened up. "I'll see you tomorrow." He nodded at Jason as he walked past and out the door.

Dez could not stop herself from crying. The stress of the day and the unknown stalker. Was he Leo? She grabbed some tissues. "I'm sorry Jason, I'm just so scared."

He closed the door and joined her. "I'm here to help. Take a deep breath. I need you to tell me everything from the beginning and show me anything suspicious."

Dez dried her eyes. "My phone is on my desk. I have some things in the drawer too. Let's sit over there." As they moved, Dez's foot caught on the edge of the supply cabinet door and she tripped. Jason caught her. Before she knew it, she hugged him tight.

Chapter 9

Leo looked around the Maintenance Services office and was satisfied all was put away and in order. He took one more proofread of his report to the District and clicked send on his District account. That was his last task for the day. Kyle had already rushed out. Fate had worked against Leo in getting to see Dez. He turned off the laptop. Maybe he'd walk out that way, one more chance to see her. Maybe they could go out for a while tonight.

He locked the office door and headed down the hall. When he realized his pace was faster than his usual relaxed saunter, he made himself slow down. No need to be anxious. He approached her class and looked through the window in the closed door. His chin dropped leaving his mouth gaping open when he recognized his love in the arms of another man. A cop. He backed away, confused.

Another door opened. Madeline's classroom. He didn't want to see anyone just now, especially Madeline. He made a quick turn and hurried in the opposite direction. As he walked out to the car, he couldn't get the vision of Dez and that man out of his head. Good thing he couldn't see her face, her beautiful, soft, face with those big, wonder-filled eyes, looking up to another man. Who was that guy? What was she doing with him after their weekend?

Sitting in his car, he pounded the steering wheel. Maybe he had her all wrong. Maybe what Madeline said was right. Dez dishonest? She cheated in her last relationship? Why was Dez telling Madeline all about our weekend anyway? That was special, between us. She had seemed so in love. Can a person pretend all that? It wasn't just what she'd said, he'd seen a look in her eyes. He shook his head and started the car engine. "I need to talk with Dez, find out what's in her heart, and find out why he was in her arms."

Madeline walked out of the school now, looking around. He decided he better get going before she spotted his car. He turned his face the other way and backed out of the space. There was Kyle sitting in his truck parked in the back of the lot. Funny, he said he was leaving at least half an hour ago. John was talking with him through the rolled down window. Leo just kept going.

He'd been looking forward to inviting Dez out tonight, that great fish and chips place down by the beach. She really seemed to like the beach. He turned out of the lot in the opposite direction. Time for a workout at the gym. A hard workout.

Chapter 10

Dez moved away from Jason. "I'm so sorry. Thanks for keeping me from falling."

Jason looked at her. "No worries. Let's see the texts on your phone and talk about what's worrying you."

Dez led him to her desk. "These are from an anonymous sender. I have no idea how to track them." She unlocked her phone and clicked on the ominous address to display the texts. Jason studied them. He took an iPad out from his vest and entered a few notes. Then he snapped a couple of pictures of the screen. "Do you have any idea what choice the sender is talking about? This one where it says, 'you have a choice to make. Choose wisely.'"

Dez shrugged. "I don't have any big decisions right now. This year I moved into my own place, and my job is going well. I'm not planning on making big life changes, at least I wasn't."

Jason looked up from his tablet directly at her. "You weren't, but now you say you are?"

Dez's cheeks warmed. "I've started dating someone new. He's really amazing and it's true love."

Jason pointed to the chair at the desk. "Maybe we should sit down, and you can tell me more."

She sat. "I've been friends with Leo. He works here on the maintenance staff. Since we started dating, it's been wonderful." As she said the words she stared at her lap.

He put the iPad on the desk. "When did you start going out?"

"Recently. It's not Leo. He wouldn't scare me. He loves me."

Jason leaned forward. "If it's not him, a few questions will clear that all up. It's better to be sure. Anything strange on your social media?"

Dez opened her desk drawer. "No, and it's not just the texts. There's this creepy stocking I found in the class this morning." She took it out and showed him the card. "I'm not even supposed to have a stocking." She pointed to the display across the room. "This is a secret Santa game for the students. I walked in this morning and found this with my name on it and that card inside. I don't even know where that picture of me came from."

Jason took out a plastic glove and bag. He studied both items, then put them in the bag and sealed it. "Unfortunately, these have been handled, but maybe we can get fingerprints. I'll take them down to the station." He stared at the open drawer. "And is that part of the decoration too?"

Dez stared at the sprig of holly and a realization hit. A lump in her throat the size of a holly berry made her hesitate. How could anyone other than Leo know about the heart shaped wreath?

When she was able to regain her voice, she explained to Jason. Her eyes teared up as he added the holly sprig to the evidence bag.

"Wait." Dez sat straight up and stared wide eyed at Jason. "On our date Saturday night, we were walking to my apartment and a black sedan tried to run us down,

Leo and me. It seemed like it was on purpose. Maybe that's the stalker?"

Jason started typing on his iPad. "Were you able to get the license number on the car? Any other description besides the color? Maybe the make or something? Could you see the driver?"

Dez slumped back in her chair. "No, it all happened so fast. I think it was a black color, but maybe dark blue. It had four doors and the back was sort of square shaped. I don't know. That's not much information, but it definitely seemed deliberate."

Jason nodded. "Did either of you report it to the police?"

Dez shook her head. "I think it could have been my ex-boyfriend. He's very upset I broke up with him and moved out. He drives by my apartment sometimes. He drives a car that could have been it. His name is Fred Sanders. If you scroll down on my phone, you'll see he texts me, but it's on his number."

Jason looked at her phone again. "I'll check him out too. He wouldn't have access to your class though, right? He couldn't have put the stocking up."

Dez paused, then said, "My ex works for the restaurant that's catering the school staff party tomorrow night. Last week some of their staff were given access to the school for planning and set up. He could be one of them."

Jason went back to his tablet. "I'll look into that. I was invited as a guest as a thank you for the police dog demonstration I did for the school. I didn't know if I'd make it because of my shift schedule, but now I'm thinking I'll make the extra effort to stop by after I get off work. Is there anything else that's happened to concern you recently?"

Dez glanced at the door next to the secret Santa display. "I've had a disagreement with two of my colleagues." She went on to describe how she'd seen Madeline stealing from the office fund and Friday's physical confrontation. "I've tried to meet with the principal again today, but no luck with busy schedules. I don't feel it's appropriate to send it on an email. I'll try to catch Mr. Milner tomorrow."

Jason typed more notes. A burst of noise came through on his radio attached to the shoulder of his vest. "Excuse me just a minute." He got up and walked over to the windows and acknowledged he heard the transmission.

This was a good opportunity to pack up her things for home. Dez felt some relief to think of relaxing at her apartment tonight, if there were no more texts. This should be such a fun time of year, instead she felt like curling up under a blanket until it all went away.

Jason sat down again. "I'll start investigating and let you know if I have any more questions. I guess I'll see you tomorrow evening at the staff party."

"Jason, there's one more thing. I've had some disagreement with John, my teaching assistant. He's the man you saw when you came in." Dez described what she'd seen by the playground gate with John and Kyle, and how John had reacted when she discussed it with him. She added that his review had some negatives in it that she'd warned him about.

Jason finished his last note, pocketed his iPad in his jacket and stood up. "Try not to worry but be cautious and safe. Let me know of any new developments. If you get another text, forward it to me." He handed her a business card. "You can reach me at this number or email me. Are you leaving now? Do you want me to walk out with you?"

"Thanks, Jason. That would be great."

Once safely in her car, she locked the doors and watched Jason take off on his motorcycle. She put her key in the ignition, but before turning it she heard her phone buzz. Dez looked all around her, in the parking lot, the playground, scanning the front of the school. Using her mirrors, she checked behind her. No one in sight. Her curiosity overwhelmed her fear and she reached for her cell. Another anonymous text. She opened it. *No worry, a cop can't stop us from being together.*

Chapter 11

It was a cold but sunny Tuesday morning and Dez left her apartment building with the frost on the doorstep, seeing her breath hang in the air before her. The dread that something else would happen with that stalker at school today consumed her. She was so sure it was Freddie, the scorn of an ex. Then yesterday, talking with Jason, doubts about dear Leo began. Her true love a stalker?

She got in her car but hesitated with the key. When Leo called last night, she almost hadn't answered. She wished she hadn't. He said he'd tried to see her all day but no luck. He'd kept a look out for her at school. He sounded confused. Had he stalked her? He wanted to see her. Terror reverberated through her and she refused. She ended the call fast. Afterward she calmed herself. Decorating her little table Christmas tree with a string of lights and ornaments had relaxed her. She looked at her apartment from the car. The tree looked cute in the window. A couple of deep breaths and the cheery sight of home revitalized her.

Somehow, she'd get through whatever lay ahead. She'd forwarded that last anonymous text to Jason. He'd find out who was behind all this. It didn't have to be Leo. She turned the key and the car roared to life.

When she walked through the open class door and saw Leo in the room her heart jumped. Was she excited to see him or scared of him? He stood with his back to her, next to the stockings display.

Madeline was in the adjoining doorway talking to him, until she saw Dez walk in. She said, "Good morning, happy Tuesday. It's getting late. I better get back before the kids come in. See you both later. You're going to the staff party tonight, right?" She didn't wait for an answer. When she walked back in her room Dez noticed the door didn't close all the way.

Leo cleared his throat. "I'm so glad to see you in person. I really enjoyed our time together Saturday night. I always enjoy being with you..."

Conscious of the possibility Madeline was listening, Dez walked to the back of the room and closed the door. Leo took her hand. "I'm confused. What's changed since Saturday? Nothing's changed for me."

She looked in his eyes and teared up at his sincere tone. "Our night was amazing. So much has happened since then. I don't know if that's changed us."

Leo looked down at their hands, then let go. "You're busy now. I heard you're seeing someone else. Is that right?"

Dez brushed a tear away. "Seeing someone? What are you talking about?"

Leo reached out to her and she looked up at him. She searched for the same look in his eyes as last weekend. She caught a glimpse of it. When he spoke again his tone was calm, quiet. "I'm not trying to upset you. Nothing should keep us apart. Can I pick you up for the staff party tonight? We can go together."

Dez took a step back. The words 'nothing should keep us apart' were so like yesterday's anonymous text.

She found the strength to shake her head. "I'm doing something after school. I'll just go to the party myself."

Leo paused, then he said, "Let's get together soon. If nothing else, we need to put together the final plans for Friday's party for the kids. Look, Dez, I don't understand why you're upset. The last thing I want to do is upset you. I'll see you at the party tonight and if you feel like it, we can talk again then."

Dez felt a little better with his nicer tone. She wanted to believe Leo was a good guy.

He took a step back. "Is the secret Santa going well? The kids talking on the playground yesterday sounded excited about it." He pointed at the back wall. "I see you have your own stocking now. Looks like someone's given you a gift inside."

Dez's jaw dropped. She was speechless. Another stocking. Her name was on it, with bigger star decorations and more glitter. And it looked like there was a lump inside. Oh no. Her feet were stuck. Her head pounded and her stomach hurt. The room swirled. That door to Madeline's, was it slightly open again? How...

Leo took her arm. "Dez, are you okay? Let me help you. Here, sit down." He guided her to the desk at the front. "I'll get you some water."

Dez reached out her hand and mumbled, "It's okay." She straightened up and saw the concerned expression on his face. "Just a headache. I'm fine. I'll take an aspirin. I need to get ready for class."

With an effort she managed to upturn her lips into a little smile. He gave her back one of his own. When he got to the door he stopped as if about to say something and gazed into her eyes. Dez was entranced by him, wishing he'd say just the right thing, so she'd know he wasn't a stalker. She didn't know what that right thing could be, but she ached to hear it.

Instead a different, familiar voice drifted in from the hall, "Excuse me."

Leo stepped out of the door and out of sight. John led in a group of children from the before school care.

Dez forced enthusiasm into her voice. "Good morning everyone."

The children greeted her, some skipped into the room. They chatted and laughed. Their happiness was contagious and warmed the chill that had paralyzed Dez, but it didn't help her headache. She grabbed the aspirin box out of her desk drawer, walked up to John with a good morning, and let him know she'd be right back. She asked him to gather all the children's ornaments for the secret Santa gifts and put them on the back counter.

The wait for morning recess seemed as long for Dez as it appeared to be for her restless students. When she was finally alone in the room, she sat at her desk and stared at that stocking. She'd texted Jason, but he'd replied that he couldn't get away and would meet her at the school later to look at it with her. She couldn't stand to ignore it all day. She had to walk back there to put the children's ornaments in the stockings anyway. She needed to get that done now.

She moved as if in the grip of some magnetic force field. She stood in front of the mystery stocking. She unhooked it. She turned it upside down over the counter and an ornament fell out. It was made from cardboard in the shape of a star. In the middle was a photo. She dropped it in horror and stifled a scream. The photo seared into her mind. It was her, putting an ornament on her little tree at home. Someone had watched her last night.

Chapter 12

Leo fought the creeping sour mood as he walked toward the maintenance office. He forced himself to make smiles for the kids headed to their classes, while his mind was in turmoil. What in the world could have changed so much in just a few days? There wasn't anything she knew about him now that she hadn't known that night. Or did she find out...or was Madeline right? Did Dez cool off because someone else hit on her? Is there someone she liked more? Or had that cop been in the picture all along and Dez had played him?

When he walked in the office Kyle was huddled over the computer. Was he surfing the net? Leo ignored it and said, "Morning. Is that the priorities for today?"

Kyle switched to a different tab. "Yep. How are you? You look stressed. You okay?"

Leo debated saying anything, then sat in the chair and crossed his arms over his chest. "Just having a bad day. Already."

Kyle turned and looked at him. "Need any help?"

Leo shook his head. "It doesn't have to do with work. It just hits me at work."

Kyle leaned back. "Oh. This sounds like woman trouble. Dez?"

Leo hesitated, then said, "It was all so good and then this week started. She's like a different person. I can't figure it out."

Kyle's laugh made Leo cringe. "Maybe she just wants more attention. Give her some flowers or something. Hey, she's friends with Madeline and she told me Dez has some kind of favorite cookie, something she really likes. Madeline said she was thinking of bringing some to the party on Friday. It's a snow cookie. No wait, snow kiss cookie. Maybe you can get some of those and sweeten her up."

Leo relaxed. Maybe something like that would at least break the ice so he could talk with her. A nice little gift. The kids had talked about snow kiss cookies being their teacher's favorite last week when she told them about the secret Santa game. Couldn't hurt. "You know Kyle, that's not a bad idea. I don't know if I can get down to Sandy's bakery before it closes tonight, but if I can, I know I'll see Dez at the staff party. I can give it to her there. Not bad, man."

Kyle nodded. "I know about the ladies. So, you're going tonight?"

Leo leaned forward. "Oh yeah. You?"

Kyle said, "Free food, what's not to like? I'll be there. Here's the list from the office. How do you want to split it up?"

It was a long day for Leo, including overtime when there was a water pipe break. After the rush when school let out, he went to his car to get some supplies he'd need for the fix. The water was turned off now that the kids were home so Leo decided to run a couple of his own quick errands too before returning to fix the pipe. As he drove toward the lot exit, he noticed Kyle standing on the edge of the playground talking with Dez's assistant John. This was starting to be a habit with them, like some kind of daily meeting. John was talking and Kyle was all attention. Leo drove the car up to the exit and looked both ways. Just before driving onto the road a motion in his mirror caught his attention. Kyle was giving John something. Something small. He couldn't see what it was.

Leo kept going. He needed to get the list of stuff for the pipes. Then he wanted to try to get to the bakery before they closed. He'd have to hurry back here to complete the fix so the caterer would have water in the kitchen. Then he needed to get home and shower and change so he'd look real good when he saw Dez tonight. Not tux good, but real good.

Chapter 13

After school, she wanted to get away. Fast. Dez drove to the beach parking lot, watching the cars behind and around her to make sure no black sedan was following. She sat in her parked car, staring past her shaking hands on the steering wheel looking over the water. She didn't want to go home. Jason's response to the terrified messages she'd left him had given her little peace. He was investigating. She checked her phone again, but nothing more from Jason. At least she'd see him tonight in person. She put her phone back in her purse, happy there weren't any new texts.

She leaned back and stared out the windshield at the bay again. It had been especially tough to announce the next secret Santa assignment. The children were so excited. They all opened their stockings and laughed and showed their ornaments to each other. She'd had to choke back her fears and give happy compliments for all the students' artwork. She shuddered over tomorrow's secret Santa assignment. She wished with all her heart that tomorrow morning there would be no new stocking for her with a poem inside.

Jason had told her that with the party tonight and lots of people around the school it's harder for someone to put anything in her room without being seen. She hardly felt like going to the party, but she didn't want to miss the opportunity to see Jason in person. And Leo. She wanted to see Leo, and she didn't want to.

She turned her head and looked at Ginardo's. It had been so fun on Saturday night. How could it become so bad so fast? On impulse she walked in for an ice cream.

Arturo greeted her from behind the counter. "Benvenuto. Welcome back. Welcome. How can I help you today?"

Dez smiled and walked over to the counter. "Ciao. Nice to see you again." She pointed at the strawberry flavor. "I'd like a small dish of this one, please."

Arturo got a scoop and a dish. "Wonderful choice. A popular flavor today." He pointed the scoop toward a table behind her. Dez turned to look and jumped with surprise to see Fred staring at her from one of the tables by the window. "Hi, Dez."

She managed a quiet, "Hello."

She turned back and paid Arturo for the ice cream she no longer craved. As she put her wallet in her purse next to her phone, she resolved to stop being tormented. A wave of anger swept through her. She took a deep breath. After thanking Arturo, she picked up her ice cream and went over to Fred's table. She gave him a hard look. "What you're doing is despicable. Stop texting me. Stop interfering with my classroom, and with my life. Stop it."

Fred's forehead wrinkled as he tilted his head. "What am I doing? I don't know what you're talking about. I got it that we're over. No hard feelings. I won't text you anything. No worries."

Dez wanted to feel relief when he said he wouldn't text, but his answer confused her. Maybe he just didn't want to admit to the rest of what he'd done. "Good. Stop leaving the—"

"Freddie!" A light giggle followed the exclamation at the door. A young blonde woman stood in a blue coat over her jeans, with a white scarf and matching wool hat. The pom pom on the top of her hat bounced up and down as she skipped across the room and sat at the table. She sat in the chair right next to him and gave him a light kiss on the lips. "Hi Freddie." She looked up at Dez. "Hello."

Dez could hardly speak, "Hello. I'd better be going. Enjoy your ice cream."

On her way out Dez paused at the door and looked back. They were huddled close, sharing his ice cream cone, and whispering together.

Arturo said to her, "Ciao. Enjoy your ice cream. See you again soon."

Dez tasted a spoonful. "Delicious. Thank you."

When she got to her car she searched for the keys in her purse. She stopped and just stared into her bag. Fred had moved on. In that case, why would he bother stalking her? She got behind the wheel.

Now she'd have to go home to get ready for the party. No. She couldn't. She'd just go as is. She sat and stared out the window as the winter darkness took over. She saw Fred and the girl come out hand in hand, chatting, walking as if they had all the time in the world. They got in the girl's car and she drove off. Dez stared down at her ice cream that had hardly melted at all as she sat in the car. She'd throw it away at the school. She wasn't hungry. The last thing she wanted to do was go back to school for a staff party, but she needed to see Jason right away. She needed to know what he'd found out.

She reached for her phone. Maybe Jason had texted her. There was a text, but not from Jason. Another message from the anonymous address. Her grip tightened on the phone as she opened it. There was a photo of her walking into Ginardo's and a caption.

You're picture perfect for me

Dez's stomach roiled with nausea. The photo was sent while she was in Ginardo's talking with Fred. Not only was Fred over her, the timing for the message wasn't right. Who sent this? If not Fred, then who? She checked that all the car doors were locked. She forwarded the text to Jason. shoved her phone back into her purse and drove away fast.

Chapter 14

The party was well underway in the school's gym. She'd gone directly there from her car, unable to force herself to stop by her classroom first. She'd ask Jason to go there with her, later. People stood around the long buffet table filled with seasonal favorites and a pretty, floral centerpiece of poinsettia plants. The caterers had gone all out with meats, breads, salads and desserts of cakes and pies. The walls boasted red and green crepe paper and balloons. Merry and warm but it cheered Dez little as she hung her coat on the rack by the door and worried.

She scanned the room for Jason. Not here yet. He said he might be late. There was a separate table set up with a punch bowl and soft drinks. Dez headed over there. She wanted to be near the door to see Jason as soon as he arrived. She filled a cup from the punch bowl and looked around again.

The catering staff bustled around the buffet replenishing serving trays. After her embarrassing run in with him, she was glad to see Fred wasn't working this event. There were people she didn't recognize, and assumed they were district administrators. Several teachers nibbled as they mingled. There was the principal. This would have been a good time to catch him, but Madeline had beat her to that idea. There she was in dedicated conversation with him. Madeline looked up and caught Dez staring at her. Madeline gave her a winning smile and held it for a moment before giving the principal her full attention again. Standing near the kitchen door and looking over the buffet, John and Kyle were talking to each other. That was getting to be quite the friendship.

She turned, and her skin tingled as Leo walked in and right up to her. He was one of the few men dressed in a suit jacket tonight. He wore a deep blue button-down dress shirt and nice tan slacks that looked new. She couldn't stop herself from a grin when she noticed the white sneakers. "Hi, Dez. Glad to see you tonight. You look great."

Amused by his admiration of the sweater and jeans she'd worn all day, her mood lightened. "Hi Leo. I didn't have time to change. You really look good."

Leo stood up a little straighter. "Here, let me fill that cup for you. Let's talk. I don't know what I did this week that's upset you, but I want to make it right. We're on holiday after Friday. Let me take you out again this weekend. We can celebrate the end of this hectic week and the beginning of time away from work. What do you say?"

All she wanted was to fall into his arms saying yes. She wanted that more than anything. How could she be sure he wasn't the creepy secret Santa stalker? "It's been a terrible week for me. I've had a secret Santa project on top of everything else." She hesitated and looked up at him. "I'd like to celebrate with you..."

Leo handed her the refilled cup. "Yes. Let's do it then. We're going to have a great time. We'll relax together. Hey, that secret Santa is a big hit. I hear the kids talking about it. They love it. Actually, I was going to bring a gift for you tonight, something..."

Jason entered the gym. The sight of his uniform turned heads. "Jason." She waved her hand at him. He walked toward her. She glanced at Leo who had stopped talking and stood staring at her.

Dez noted what he'd just said. He was going to bring her a gift. A creepy, stocking gift? "I've been waiting for Jason to get here."

Jason said, "Hi, Dez."

She said, "I'm glad to see you. This is Leo."

Leo gave an abrupt nod. "Nice to meet you."

Jason picked up a soda from the table. "Glad to meet you too. I just got off my shift. It was nice of them to invite me as a thank you for the police dog demo I did for the kids. Are you a teacher here too?"

Leo put his hands on his hips. "Right. I remember that assembly. The kids loved the dog. I'm on the maintenance staff. I started here during summer school."

Jason popped the top on his soda. "Nice of them to have a party for the staff."

Dez shifted from one foot to the other. Leo seemed stiff now, so unlike him. Was he nervous around a cop because he's a stalker? "Jason, I wanted to talk with you about something." She looked from Jason to Leo, then she glanced down at the floor and back at Jason.

Leo threw his cup in the trash at the end of the table. "I think I'll go fill up a plate. Dez, do you want something." She shook her head. He took a step closer to her and touched the back of her hand. "You're sure? Why don't I surprise you with something? I'll be right back."

Dez moved close to Jason. Her voice faltered as she whispered, "The texts and gifts are getting scarier. Seeing Leo tonight is hard for me. I don't want it to be him. He asked me out for this weekend, but then he said he was bringing a gift for me."

Jason looked down at her. "We don't have enough information yet to identify who the stalker is. It's good to be cautious but try to stay calm."

Dez hadn't realized her stress showed. She relaxed her tensed shoulders and rubbed her hands over her face. She looked around the gym. "Maybe we could just go check my class while he's at the buffet. I don't know if I can face him again." Jason motioned with his hand for her to wait. "The two men by the door in the corner. It looks like that leads to the kitchen. That's John your assistant, right? Who's the other guy? The one pointing to the plate of cookies on the table?"

"That's Kyle. He works in maintenance too."

Jason said, "Looks like Leo is going for some of the cookies. He may have to fight off that other man. Look at him standing at the table filling up his own plate with cookies. Now he's popping a couple in his mouth."

Dez tapped her foot. "That's Joe Prescott, the music teacher."

Jason muttered, "He'll have to do some miles with the marching band to work off all those calories."

Dez abruptly turned her back to the buffet table. "Uh oh, Leo's coming back."

Jason looked down at her. "It's okay. Take it easy."

There was a loud crash by the kitchen doorway that startled people including Dez. She looked to see what happened. The server rushed to pick up the platter that fell off the table. He picked up the scattered cookies on the floor and put them in a trash bag.

Leo handed her a paper plate. "Looks like I got these just in time for you, Dez. They're your favorite snow kiss cookies."

Jason looked across the room. "If you'll excuse me, I just want to go thank your principal again for the invitation tonight." Dez cleared her throat and shook her head, but Jason continued. "I'll be right back."

Leo stared at her. "Would you like one?"

Dez looked down at the cookies, and chuckled.

Leo gave her a friendly smile. "I like to hear you laugh. Cookies make you happy?"

The sound of his voice was soothing, the sound of a friend. "It's silly. These are glazed. There's a story behind snow kiss cookies and they have powdered sugar."

"That's important?"

"In the story there's just enough powder to sweeten each bite and leave extra on the lips to share in a kiss." Dez's face flamed with heat.

She stepped over to put the plate down on one of the chairs by the door. Leo followed her and stood close as she abruptly turned back right into his arms. They lingered, then remembering where they were, Dez took a step back from his embrace. "The cookies... It's a cute legend my grandmother told me when I was little."

Leo coaxed her, "Tell it to me."

Those dark brown eyes searing into her soul were irresistible. "It's about Emma and William who lived in Denmark hundreds of years ago. They were best friends. Once upon a time in adulthood, on a cold December day Emma rushed out to find her family's horse. The animal had broken free from the barn and wandered into the forest. A terrible snowstorm kicked up. Emma fell and hurt her ankle and couldn't get home."

Leo groaned. "Poor Emma."

Dez was tickled he paid attention to her story. "A nisse told William she was missing."

Leo cocked his head to the side with his endearing grin. "What's a nisse?"

Dez winked. "Of course, that's a cross between a gnome and a Santa."

Leo laughed. "Of course."

Dez continued her story. "They're Danish magical beings. The nisse led William through the storm to Emma. As they approached, a fierce wolf raced to attack her. William grabbed a hefty fallen branch and beat the wolf away."

"Bravo!" Leo cheered.

Dez smiled and in it she felt a longing. "The two friends reunited with a warm hug. The snowstorm subsided into a light flurry of flakes."

Leo asked, "So she was okay?"

"Yes, but she was hungry. The nisse took out a decorated bag from his satchel and inside was a koekje. That means 'little cake' in Danish. That's where we get our word cookie."

Leo said, "I didn't know that."

Dez went on with the story, "As the nisse offered the koekje, snowflakes fell and frosted the top. Emma and William each took a bite, then they laughed to see powdered snow on each other's lips like a kiss. That's when they realized..."

"Realized what?"

Dez looked deep in his eyes, searching. "They realized they loved each other." She looked down at his sneakers. "The nisse knew it all along and shouted 'Forelsket' meaning in love. That's why he gave them the Snow Kiss Cookies"

Leo put his hand under her chin, and she gazed up at him. The look he gave her back was like they were the only two people in the room. "I love the sparkle in your eyes from that story." Then he broke the spell. "Instead of a Santa stocking I should give you gifts from a nisse satchel."

Secret Santa stockings? Was that about the creepy gifts? No! A surge of panic moved her. She couldn't make a scene in front of this room full of colleagues, the principal, people from the district. "Leo, please excuse me. I promised Jason to show him my class."

Dez waved at Jason and rushed out the exit, hoping he followed, and Leo didn't. She looked back. Jason was coming her way and behind him Madeline stood next to Leo talking. Dez hurried down the hall.

Once out of sight of the gym she slowed, and Jason caught up. Dez put her hand on the class doorknob, but Jason guided her aside. "Let me go in first, just in case we surprise someone."

She whispered, "The light switch is on this wall, on the left of the door as you walk in."

As Jason turned on the light, she peered into an empty room. She grabbed his arm and pointed to the back of the room. "There's a new stocking on the wall again."

Tears rolled down her face as they walked to the stocking. Jason took an evidence bag from a pocket of his vest and put on clear plastic gloves as well. He unhooked the stocking. "There's a piece of paper inside." He put the paper in the clear bag, then he hung the stocking back up again. "Just putting it back temporarily."

The stationary looked computer generated with a border of alternating Santa and stocking. Dez said, "The gift for the children to bring tomorrow is to write a holiday poem. Is that what it is?"

Jason scanned the paper and frowned. "Sort of."

She leaned against the counter, wiping away tears with a tissue. "I can't read it. Will you read it to me?"

"Okay. Brace yourself.

Come sit on secret Santa's knee

Because I am your destiny.

Now that I have found you dear

I will always keep you near.

You'll do exactly as I say

When I decide to come to play...

Soon"

"Oh my God Jason. I'm so scared."

"Be strong, Dez. We're going to catch this guy. I'll take these in for evidence. There may be fingerprints. It's printed from a computer, maybe we can track something with the font. I'll check the surveillance cameras for this evening too. Hopefully there's a camera on your hallway. The detectives are on this too."

"Jason, do you think it's Leo? I was on his boat Saturday night. Oh God, he could have locked me in there and sailed away and no one would have ever found me." Dez shook all over.

Jason put a hand on her shoulder. "He didn't. You're okay. You've got to keep your guard up though. Be careful the situations you put yourself in. Your Saturday night worked out, but I'm keeping Leo on my suspect list. I'm also investigating your assistant John. He certainly has opportunity and there's the disagreements you've had. His association with Kyle is curious too, the way that you described it. It may or may not have to do with this harassment, and it may be illegal activity. It could be innocent, but it is suspicious."

Dez said, "There's the fight with Madeline too, and unfortunately this adjoining door has no lock. It all sounds like a creepy guy is doing this, but it could be her making it look like that to scare me more. She threatened me the other day. She wanted to scare me."

Jason said, "I'm checking into her too. I followed up about your ex, Fred. You may not be aware that he bought a car after trading in his old sedan. He's driving a jeep. He made the deal a couple of months ago."

Dez listened with interest. "Really? All this time I assumed it was him driving past my apartment, it was someone else."

Jason said, "I'm tracking who bought the car, but it doesn't look like it was Fred who tried to run you over Saturday night."

Dez shook her head. "I was sure all this was Fred until I saw him after school today. He's seeing a girl and they look happy, like they've been together for a while. They were having fun. He's over me."

Jason picked up the bag with the stocking and zipped it in an inside pouch of his vest along with the one with the poem. "I'll remain vigilant with Fred, but he seems least likely. He has limited access to the school. How would he even know about your secret Santa lesson plan, let alone find a way to put the daily gift on a hook in your class? Hey, that's a siren."

The two of them looked out the window. There was a foreboding red then blue throbbing in the heavy mist. The screech got louder, and suddenly an ambulance with lights flashing raced into the parking lot and sped up to the doorway. Paramedics rushed into the school.

Chapter 15

Dez followed Jason as he pushed past the onlookers to the medics. One of them knelt over a man writhing on the floor in obvious pain. Joe Prescott, a sugary glaze visible on his mustache.

Dez recognized Joe's wife answering the paramedic's questions. "He felt fine all day. We came to the party early to help with decorations. Joe had lots of energy. He set up the streaming background music on the speaker system. He was so happy."

The medic frowned. "Did you notice what he was eating?"

"He enjoyed a few of the cookies before they spilled on the floor. He's always loved desserts." Her lip trembled as she asked, "Is he going to be okay?"

The medic answered, "He's getting the best of care. We're going to take him into Bayside Hospital. You can ride with us."

Jason moved the crowd back and they wheeled Joe out on a stretcher, his wife in tow. The shock impacted the party and people began saying goodbyes. Dez took Jason by the hand and led him past Leo and the others who remained.

Dez was intent on her purpose. "I overheard his wife talking. She said he was eating the cookies before he felt sick. He ate a bunch of them. Remember the rest got thrown away in the trash? There's something wrong with those cookies, the ones Leo gave me."

The catering staff cleared the leftovers and broke down the table. Jason looked in the trash can he'd seen the cookies dumped into, but the plastic lining was empty. He stopped one of the staff and asked him where the trash was taken.

"Tonight's trash is still in the corner of the kitchen waiting to go out to the dumpster. We do that last thing before we leave."

Jason motioned to Dez. "Wait here. I'm going to look through and get those cookies. I don't want you leaving on your own. I'll take you home. I want to check that your apartment is safe. This won't take long."

Dez scanned the gym. Some of the remaining partiers, including Leo were taking down decorations and cleaning up the gym. She remembered the cookies Leo had offered her. The plate still sat on the chair by the door. Were they poisoned? Dez made a quick decision to grab them. Jason could have them examined too. She saw Leo head in that direction. Had he spotted the plate? Was he going to hide them? John and Kyle were on their way out, but Madeline had stopped them to talk. Dez moved quickly. She scooped up the plate, wrapped the cookies in the napkin underneath and shoved them into her coat pocket just as Leo reached her.

"I hope Joe's okay. He's such a nice guy."

Dez muttered, "Me too."

"Clean-up is going fast. I can take that plate. I've got a trash bag here."

She dropped the plate in. "Thanks."

Kyle came up behind Leo. He stared at Dez with a strange expression of contempt. He talked to Leo while his gaze stayed on her. "Hey, all good. I'm taking off. I'll be in early tomorrow and give the floor a final mop."

Leo turned around to answer. "Okay. See you tomorrow."

Kyle gave a wave. "Night, Dez."

She fidgeted with the strap on her purse. "Good night." She stared at his back as he walked off.

Leo was talking to her. "... if you can wait, I'll be right back and walk you to your car. Maybe we can get a coffee or something?"

Dez shook her head. "I'm tired. I'm just going home. Oh, there's Jason."

Jason walked up to them empty handed. "Ready to go, Dez? I'll follow you in my car."

"Ready."

She heard Leo as she walked out the door. "I'll see you tomorrow, Dez."

Jason was quiet as they hurried to their cars. When she got to her apartment, he stopped his squad car behind her. They stood, and he shook his head. "None of those trash bags had the cookies."

"What?"

"Someone found a way to sneak them out of there. I even looked out in the dumpster. When I asked the staff about the cookies, they told me someone at the party brought that platter because they didn't supply cookies."

A shudder went up Dez's spine. "That's odd. It wasn't a potluck."

"I don't know yet who brought them. I called it into the station. They're going to do a more thorough search tonight. On the way here I checked with the hospital and Joe Prescott is in ICU."

Dez took the napkin out of her coat pocket. "These are the ones Leo gave me. They were still on the bench, and I grabbed them."

Jason hurried to get out an evidence bag. "Good thinking. Let me check your apartment, and then I'll get these to the lab."

Dez took out her cell phone. "I just got a text." She typed in her pin and the screen lit up both their faces in the night. "Oh no."

"What does it say?"

"How did you like the party? Sorry you missed dessert."

Chapter 16

Midweek. Leo looked forward to vacation and reconnecting with Dez. He walked into the maintenance office. There was Kyle huddled over the small screen of the computer again. The big screen was off. "Morning Kyle. Anything left to clean up in the gym? Should I head over there?"

Kyle stopped typing and switched screens. "Gym's all done. It just needed a quick mop."

"Thanks. I've been wanting to look at that dishwasher in the kitchen that Gene complained about, so I guess I'll check on that."

"I'll do the assessment on the playground equipment."

Leo took his jacket off and put it in his locker. Kyle went back to the computer. Leo was tempted to go past Dez's room, but he stifled that urge and took the other route to the cafeteria. Focus on work would help him.

The cafeteria kept him busy all morning. Once he fixed the dishwasher Gene had several other small tasks ready and waiting for him. It kept his mind engaged, his hands busy, and his sense of humor fully in force. Gene was always a great joker. By the time he'd finished, the students were lining up for lunch. The kids waved and said hi to Leo. Some stopped him to chat. It warmed his heart whenever he got time with the kids.

Eventually he left the cafeteria and, as he walked down the hall, Madeline waved him down. "Leo, so glad I ran into you. I've been looking for someone. I need to temporarily move this bookshelf. We're doing a musical lesson this afternoon and we need a bigger space. Could you help me?"

"Sure. Lead the way."

He followed her, hoping she wouldn't start talking about Dez again. He'd get the bookcase moved and make an excuse to get out of there.

"It's this one. I want to move it in front of the adjoining door. We can move it back again at afternoon recess."

"You're sure that's the best spot? We could just shift it here behind..."

"Yes, this is fine. I'll just quickly let Dez know not to come through here for a couple of hours." Madeline opened the door wide. There was Dez standing close to Jason. They were talking and looking at something he was holding. Leo froze like an outdoor pipe. His improved mood vanished.

Madeline leaned forward. "Oh Dez, sorry to interrupt. I wanted to let you know not to use the door for a couple of hours. I'm going to have it blocked for a lesson after lunch, but I'll free it up again later this afternoon. Okay?"

Dez said, "Sure. I'll put a couple of chairs in front of it so there's no accidents."

Madeline looked back at Leo, then at Dez again. "Thanks so much." She closed the door.

Leo helped her with the bookcase as if in a fog and then got out of there fast. Jason with Dez again? What's going on between the two of them? He hoped the maintenance office would be empty, but it wasn't.

Kyle said, "Madeline came looking for you."

Leo kept his temper in check. "I just came from there. The cafeteria took longer than I expected so I'm going on lunch now."

Kyle said, "No sweat. I'll be here."

Leo grabbed his jacket out of his locker and took a long walk. He debated it in his mind. He didn't want to betray anyone, and this could lead to that. On the other hand... He made a decision. He vowed to do it after work today.

Chapter 17

No stalling, Leo made a quick exit after the school day and headed into downtown Bayside. Now he sat at a table in the café, nursing the coffee he'd ordered and watching the gal cleaning up behind the counter. There was only one other group at a table, four women finishing their drinks. He considered how he'd start his conversation, assuming Katherine Watson came in. He looked out the window. Rain had started again. A wet, black cat showing a distinct frown trotted across the patio toward the house. It looked determined to get out of the weather.

The foursome was standing now. Katherine had joined them. She chatted with the ladies, then said to the barista, "Better cover the gift shop. I can take over here until MJ gets back."

That was his cue. Leo moved onto a stool at the bar. "Hi Katherine. I haven't seen you for a while. How are you?"

"Leo, what a nice surprise. It has been a while. The school must keep you busy."

"It's a great place to work."

Katherine seemed to relax a little as she leaned on the counter. "I bet it takes a lot of energy to keep up with the kids."

Leo played with his coffee cup. "Katherine, I came today because I was hoping to talk with you. You're good friends with Dez. I'm also good friends with Dez. Last weekend we went out again and we moved beyond friends. It seemed like we were both so close. Suddenly she runs cold to me, and then just as suddenly a spark flickers and heats up, but then goes out again. I wouldn't normally ask, but can you shed any light on what's going on? Has she said anything to you about us?"

Leo stopped himself from blabbering on. She stood straight up again. "Really, she hasn't said much to me. I know she did enjoy your time together last weekend, but you already know that. Even if she had talked with me, I wouldn't feel comfortable repeating that to you. Don't you think this is a conversation you should have with her?"

He nodded. "I've tried." He drank out of his cup as he debated one more time in his head whether to say more. He watched Katherine pick up a towel and wipe the counter. He decided to say more. "I've been surprised to see Jason at the school this week. He's been there a few times. Each time he's been with Dez. I didn't know they're friends."

Katherine put the towel in a hamper behind her. "Jason's been working a case at the school."

"You mean last night, about Mr. Prescott..."

"Oh no, his case started before then."

Leo brightened hearing that. He leaned forward eager to hear more. "You mean the case has been all week? He's questioning all the teachers? He's not dating Dez?"

Leo shut up and stifled a broad smile away from Katherine's probing scrutiny. "I don't know how he's investigating, but as far as I know Jason and I are still dating."

"Right. Of course. Yes. He's been tracking something illegal. What is it?" Leo's thoughts turned immediately to John and Kyle.

"You know that the music teacher was sick? Rob Thompson reported in this afternoon's news that he's being treated for poisoning from what he ate at the school last night. Do you bake, Leo?"

Katherine's dark brown eyes examined him, bore into his gaze. Was she interrogating him? Was someone trying to kill teachers? Did she think it was him? Was someone trying to kill Dez? His whole body tensed. "I didn't bake last night. Is Dez in danger?"

She said, "I don't know any details. Have you been texting her?"

Leo put his hand up to his forehead, confused. "Texting? I've been trying to talk with her at school in person, but she's avoiding me. Why didn't she tell me this? She must be scared."

He shook his head. Why did this woman just keep staring at him? He gulped the last of his drink and blurted it all out. "Dez is the most beautiful woman I've met. Not just her looks. I'm in love with the person she is. I'd do anything for her." He looked Katherine in the eyes. "I'd do anything to protect her if she's in danger. If I'm not the one for her then I'd step aside and away from her. I don't want anything bad to happen to her."

He felt that intense stare sweep over him again. Was she evaluating his sincerity? It was a long pause, but Leo waited it out.

She sighed and put her hands on her hips. "Have you heard about her secret..."

He jumped in, "The secret Santa fun for the kids. Yes. It ends with the party Friday."

He sat still as she watched him. "Did she tell you someone has been giving her something every day too?

Leo shook his head. "No, she didn't say that. So, the case started with the holiday plans last week?"

Katherine said, "It's been scary for her. She doesn't know who it is, and what they gave her made her contact Jason."

Leo stood up. "Thanks, Katherine. I have to go."

She raised her voice. "Wait, what are you going to do?"

Leo stopped and looked at her. "I don't know yet. I'm going to think about it tonight. She may not want to see me, but I'm going to help her."

Chapter 18

Dez parked her car and reached for her purse. How she dreaded going into class. She groaned. Yesterday's assignment was for the children to string friendship bracelets from packets of beads. Was there going to be a stocking for her again? With a bracelet inside? Where was Jason? She grabbed her phone. A text from him. Oh no, he was supposed to be here this morning and check the class with her. She read it. He was delayed at the station and would be here as soon as possible. It was sent ten minutes ago.

Leo's car pulled into the next space. Her hand shook, and her pulse quickened. After she got out, he did the same. He looked over the roof of his car with a good morning and a disarming smile.

Leo stood still. "I've just found out a little about what you've been going through. Katherine told me teachers are being threatened. You're being threatened. I'm so sorry. Let me know what I can do to help you."

Her eyes watered. She couldn't look at him. She walked forward. When she got to the school entrance she stopped at the door, and she felt him next to her. His voice was quiet now. "You're having trouble trusting anyone. I understand. I'll do whatever you think will help."

Dez wanted to believe him. Jason had said to stay away from dangerous situations. She looked at Leo. She heard sincerity in his words, and love. In desperation she blurted out, "Why did you give me those cookies last night?"

His forehead wrinkled and his head tilted as he started to reach his hand out. Then he put it back at his side. "The cookies? I just wanted to bring you a treat to cheer you up. I was going to get your favorite cookies at the bakcry but didn't have time to get there. When I got to the table Kyle and John pointed at the plate and said those were the kind you like. That's the only reason."

Juggling her mixed emotions, she went through the door. They walked together in silence. When they got in the class Dez felt him looking at her. She checked the display in the back. Tears fell as her fears were realized. There was a new stocking with her name on it. She looked at him. "Why?"

Leo followed her look. "What is it?"

She pointed to the back and started walking. She unhooked it and tipped it upside down. A silver bracelet tumbled onto the counter. It had a single charm. It was heart shaped with a crack through it and a tiny silver axe embedded in the top. She looked from it to Leo.

His jaw had dropped open. "Someone sneaked in here to leave this?"

She said, "Something every day this week."

When Leo reached for it Dez stopped him. "Don't. There might be fingerprints. Jason needs to look at it." She searched in her purse until she found a pen. She used that to hook the silver chain and the charm flipped over. It was engraved. Leo's grip on her hand tightened. She read the single word.

He asked her, "What does 'soon' mean?"

As she described the poem, his eyes got wider, and his usual grin was replaced by a tight-lipped line and a stiff chin. She described the other gifts too.

"Dez, you need to contact Jason right away."

She took out her phone. "He was supposed to be here by now, but he's running late."

Leo let go of her hand. "Text him a picture of it. Or call him."

The phone vibrated in her hand. They both looked at it light up. Leo said, "Maybe that's Jason."

Dez opened the texts and gasped. It was another anonymous text. She looked around the room and out the window.

Leo helped her sit down. "What's the matter?"

She was crying again. "The stalker texts me."

Leo put his arm around her, and they looked at her phone. They read it together.

I'm charmed by you. See you soon, forever.

Dez dropped the phone in her lap. Leo picked it up. She watched him scroll, and she knew he was reading all the messages. The wrinkles in his frowning expression increased from somber to full alarm. His usual endearing grin turned upside down. "I'll stay with you until Jason gets here. You're not safe. Let's go to the office and tell the principal what's going on, and you're not teaching today."

She sat up and wiped away her tears. "The children. They can't see me like this. I have to get myself together." She took some deep breaths.

Leo bent down in front of her chair. "Dez this is dangerous, for the kids too. We need to get the office involved. Leave Jason a message that you'll meet him there."

"I can't just leave the class unattended. Now, I have to get ready." She tried to ignore his protests as she used the pen in her shaking hand to get the bracelet into the stocking then put that in her desk drawer.

John walked in and said good morning. "I've got the reading lesson ready to go for today. It's still on for this afternoon, right?"

Dez sat down at her desk. She'd forgotten all about John's lesson, and here he was showing enthusiasm for it. She mentally scolded herself for not staying on task. She adjusted her voice. "Yes, of course it's still on. I'm looking forward to it. Anything you need from me?"

"No, I've really got it together. I'm heading down to get the morning day care kids now."

"Thanks, John." Dez saw Leo in the back of the room pointing to the windows. A police car pulled up. Leo moved to her desk. "It's okay Leo. Jason will know what to do. You better get to your own work."

Leo looked out the window again and then back at her. "Text me if you need anything. I'll check on you later. I'll go as soon as he gets in here." He gently rested his hand over hers.

John returned and Jason walked in behind the group of children. Dez asked John to watch the class until she got back. She told him to collect their secret Santa bracelets, and if she was late to go ahead and start them with a spelling game. John eyed Jason and stuttered that he would take care of it. As Leo left the room, he said to Jason, "Glad you're here."

Dez grabbed the stocking and hid it down at her side as she walked out. "Let's go to the teacher's lounge." She handed him her phone. "I got this right after I opened the new stocking."

Jason studied the screen as they went into the empty lounge and sat down on one of the couches. "Another stocking today then? Maybe there's something on the new surveillance camera." He put his plastic gloves on and examined the bracelet. "Sorry I wasn't here earlier."

"It's okay. Leo was with me." She described all that happened.

"Dez, he's not off the suspect list, but I will say the detectives haven't surfaced any red flags on him."

She hunched over and held her stomach as he filled the evidence bag. "That still leaves John and Madeline."

Jason sealed the bag. "John has access, and he knows the lesson plans. He lives at home with his mother and grandmother. His mother drives a black sedan. His grandmother is an invalid and they care for her. It appears he's getting her naturopathic and herbal medicines. I think that may have something to do with the times you saw him with Kyle, what they may be handing each other."

Dez said, "His attitude toward work and the kids is improving, I think. I didn't know he was helping take care of his grandmother."

Jason leaned forward. "We're looking closely at Kyle. He has access to your class. He's a loner from what we've found. There's an added dimension to him with his potential knowledge for supplying herbals to Kyle. You'll find out from the news later today, Joe Prescott died early this morning. It was a poison in the cookies. We're not saying any more about that now, but it may be something Kyle could have put together. He drives a truck every day, but there is a black sedan parked on his property."

Jason referred to his iPad. "The detectives looked into Madeline. That argument you had where you felt she was on the verge of violence concerns me. She has a police record of complaints from neighbors where she used to live, and even from a neighborhood store. She has a handgun registered to her. Indications are it's a man behind this, but she could be wording the texts and notes that way to hide her identity. She has access to her brother's black car, but it's not a sedan."

Her eyes teared up. "That's terrible about Joe. He was so nice. His poor family."

Jason stood up. "I was at the hospital when he died. I talked with his wife a little yesterday. Dez, today I was late because I was waiting on final authorization and clearance from your principal. We're posting an officer at the school until we've caught the killer. I'm on the first shift. I'll radio that I have evidence for pick up, then I'll go out and get Hobbs. I want the dog as an added precaution. This decision will make it easier to question people and to pick up more clues. And of course, we'll be on the spot if something happens."

Dez nodded, dazed. "Okay." It all seemed too real now. Overwhelming.

Chapter 19

Friday morning's bright, cloudless sky inspired strength in Dez on her drive to school. Last day before holiday and she resolved to be optimistic. Jason patrolling the halls with Hobbs was sure to solve this mystery.

She didn't know about John now. He'd shown so much improvement in such a short time. More energy. More enthusiasm. His reading lesson yesterday afternoon was wonderful. His idea for each child to read a page out loud followed by everyone recognizing each of them with John's invented fun cheer had brought extra effort all around. So many of the students commented they liked the reading circle, and John seemed motivated too. He'd actually blushed after class when she'd complimented his lesson. She needed to give him more responsibility. Maybe she'd been wrong about him when it came to teaching. Maybe she'd been wrong thinking he might be the stalker too.

She stopped at the red light and relished the best, most hopeful news of the day. Despite Jason's warnings to be cautious, Dez felt no doubt about Leo now. It felt so good to realize that. She said it out loud, "I have no doubt about Leo." An amazing calm vibrated through her soul. "I'm happy. I'm in love." The light turned green. She drove forward. It would be wonderful to see Leo today.

She mentally reviewed the day ahead and the tasks she needed to complete in time for the party. She was glad she was early. The children were sure to be over-stimulated all morning in anticipation. Thank goodness for a half day dismissal. She turned into the lot and parked. She'd only expected one police car, Jason's. There was one in a visitor spot, and two more parked by the main entrance.

As she walked down the hall to her class, her heart skipped a beat and then pounded in her ears when a hand from behind landed on her shoulder. Then she recognized the deep, comforting voice. It soothed her fear. She faced Leo. "So, they said to keep back for now. Better wait here, with me."

She looked down the hall at her open class door. "What's going on?"

Leo said, "They think they've got the stalker. Your nightmare is over."

Dez clasped her hands together in great hope. "Thank God. How? Who?"

"I don't know, but I was nearby and looked in. I overheard some things as more cops arrived. They think it's Madeline."

Dez listened closely. "Madeline?"

Leo said, "That's what they think. They're taking her in for questioning. Jason found her in your room early this morning. She had a stocking in her hand. I don't know if there was anything inside it. I overheard she has a history of threatening on social media too."

Dez looked toward her room again. "She acted pretty violent toward me one day, but it's hard to believe she'd be that upset to really want to hurt me."

Leo said, "It's hard to believe she's behind it, but she may have been caught in the act. There's enough evidence so they're going to take her to the station. Oh, here they come."

Dez couldn't take her eyes off the sight of Madeline with hands behind her back, escorted by two officers and shouting, "I found that stocking. I didn't make it. I didn't do anything."

Leo pulled Dez gently toward him as the trio walked past them. Madeline stared at Dez and screamed, "You! You framed me."

The officers kept her moving, and they disappeared out the main door. Dez hurried to her room but Jason stopped her before she could go in. He gave a quick tug on Hobbs' leash and the dog immediately sat. "We need to finish gathering evidence. I advised the principal it's best to conduct your class today in a different room. Check in with him. Be happy, Dez. It looks like we've got your perpetrator. We'll know more soon."

Dez hesitated. She wasn't sure if she could really smile again. Was it all over? She petted Hobbs behind the ear. "Thank you, Jason. I'll get to the office and find John, then we'll intercept the kids and steer them to the right place."

One of the officers called Jason. As he walked away with Hobbs, Dez stretched forward for a glimpse inside. Some of the desks were scattered across the back of the room. The adjoining door was wide open. An officer was taking pictures, and another was closely examining the back counter. Then another officer appeared before her and closed the door.

Chapter 20

This calm and sense of fun had not been a part of Dez for a long week. Now she could relax and enjoy her students. It was time for elation, no more fear. Leo and Kyle had worked fast to set up the cafeteria for class. It was a great use of space for a half day with no lunches.

In a quick re-think of the holiday party logistics, the principal agreed it would be most helpful if John and Leo would take the kids out for recess while Rachel and Dez set up the party treats and decorations in the gym. Kyle could cover maintenance needs. Dez savored the joyous festivities, and Leo's invitation for dinner tonight.

Just before recess all the secret Santa identities were revealed with a game John created. At the peak of the excitement Leo arrived and with John they escorted the kids as they skipped out to play. Dez enjoyed the immediate silence in the room after they left. She grabbed the box of decorations and moved to the gym. Kyle was there.

He shut the door to the kitchen. "Rachel had an emergency with one of the kids and had to go. She asked me to help you."

Dez put the box on a table. "Okay, well it won't take long to put these few decorations out. If you want to start, I'll go back to the kitchen and start bringing the treats in."

Kyle blocked her way. He stood immovable in front of the closed door and glared down on her with bloodshot eyes and a fury that made her think of the cracked heart charm and its axe hitting the target. He cut the air with one word, "No."

A chill went up Dez's spine and her stomach clenched. Blood drained from her face despite pounding in her veins. This couldn't be happening. Madeline was the stalker.

He spoke again, "Santa's here, baby. Come give me a kiss. We're going away together now. We have to hurry."

Dez willed her feet to move. She darted toward the main exit. Kyle was faster. He tackled her and they both fell hard on the floor. She felt sick to her stomach as he wrapped himself around her and held her tight. His hot breath blasted onto her face and slit eyes bore into her. "You naughty girl. You're coming with me."

She screamed. He muffled her screams with his hand as she struggled to get away. She could hardly move, fighting to breathe.

He seethed into her ear, "I asked you out first. You said no dating coworkers. He works here too. You're going out with me all right. Today we die together."

She pushed away. His grip across her mouth tightened as he jerked her against him again. She kicked him hard and hit with her fists. She bit his hand. He rolled her on her back and pressed her against the floor. She lay immobile as he loomed over her. She clamped her lips shut and shook her head back and forth violently, kicking and fighting him with the last of her strength. He put his hands around her neck and choked her. She couldn't breathe. Gasping and gagging she fought for any air, for any life. She couldn't think. She couldn't breathe. She blacked out.

Dez didn't know how long she'd remained in the dark, but now there was a light. A fuzziness. Life expanded her lungs. She slowly realized she was in the gym. Kyle sat on the floor stuffing glazed cookies in his mouth. She moved feebly, coughed, and groaned. He froze and stared at her. She tried to get up, but her strength failed. He was on top of her again. Cookie crumbs fell on her as he wrapped his hands around her throat.

Chapter 21

Leo kneeled to tie Ronna's laces into double knotted bows, so they'd stop coming undone. The little girl was happily chattering to him about Peter being her secret Santa. She showed Leo her beaded friendship bracelet. It didn't surprise him when Ashley joined them. These two stuck together like a nut and bolt, Ashley being the adorable nut to Ronna's grounded personality. They proved the fun of variety in life.

Leo finished the bow and looked up. "Hi Ashley, nice of you to come over. Ronna your shoes are tied."

Ronna checked them. "Thank you."

Ashley's eyes twinkled as she brought her coated arm and mittened hand onto his shoulder. "I knight you Sir Kind Man."

Leo stood up and did a deep bow with a flourish. "I'm honored, fair princess."

The girls giggled. "Come on Ronna, let's go down the slide again."

Leo watched them run off, then scanned the grounds checking on others. Some kids played four-square on the pavement, and others were intent on hopscotch. He was surprised to see Rachel talking with John.

He moved closer to them. "Rachel, everything set up already?"

"I was in the gym. Kyle said John needed me out here. He stayed to help Dez instead, and here I am."

John said, "I didn't ask for you, but glad you're here. I wanted to tell you about the math feature Dez is planning for when we come back in January..."

Leo listened to John until he saw Toby fall in a game of tag on the grass. He stepped forward, but Toby got up and back in the game. Leo's stare lingered to be sure all was well with Toby, then he focused on the gate in the background. Kyle and John had stood there together, and in other places.

Leo felt uneasy. "Hey John, you and Dez have a lot of activities in your class. You talk about it with all the other teachers?"

John looked at him. "If they're interested. Madeline asked me questions because she's got a first-grade class like us. I had an idea Rachel might..."

Leo stepped closer. "You and Kyle get together at work sometimes. Did you talk to him about your class plans?"

John tilted his head. "I mean, we talk some work. He was interested in the holiday activities because of his cleaning up the room. He asked about the stockings and stuff."

Leo crossed his arms. They talked every day. John told him about the stockings. The gifts? Kyle could get in the room anytime for maintenance. He'd been busy on the computer and printer. Printing photos maybe? Now Kyle's all alone with Dez. Leo wasn't a person to jump to conclusions, but he acted on feelings and these facts all fit.

Leo started moving and shouted, "Call 911." Rachel took her phone out of her pocket. "Tell them they've got the wrong person. Tell them a woman is under attack in the gym. Now." Leo moved past them and sprinted for the building.

He pushed on the gym door. It didn't budge. He threw himself against it several times. Jason turned into the hall just as the door gave way. Leo ran in. There was Kyle. Scumbag. Sitting over Dez on the ground, keeping her down, choking her. Fury surged through Leo. His hands hardened into fists. He'd never felt heart pounding rage like this. He leaped at Kyle and threw him off her, hitting him with all his strength. Someone grabbed him by the arm and pulled him off Kyle. Jason yelled a command and Hobbs snarled at Kyle who was on the ground, bleeding.

Leo shook Jason off him and ran to Dez.

"Dez. Dez." Leo cradled her in his lap. There was no life in her eyes. No expression on her face. Her lips were still. Leo checked for her pulse. He had to feel something. Then her head moved. Her eyes fluttered. She gasped. He saw only her in the gym. He never wanted to let her go.

Chapter 22

Dez had been devastated by the attack, but her spirits soared when the school nurse, and especially when the paramedics cleared her. Body aches, bruising on her neck already, and a scraped knee left her moving slow. She cringed at the pain in her arms where he'd held her down. Tears again. A horrible attack. She was lucky to be alive. She took a deep breath. She quietly rejoiced with a whispered, "I'm alive."

She slowly stepped out of the nurse's office, and there was Leo waiting for her. When she'd come conscious again, he'd been the first person she saw. Jason had said that Leo saved her life. He stood up with a broad grin and a wink. "How are you doing? Do you feel up to saying happy vacation to your students before they go home?"

"Absolutely."

"Somehow I knew you'd want to. We moved the party outdoors, away from the...emergency. Chilly but sunny. Let me help you out there. Don't want you to overdo it."

It felt good to see her students. She wished them all happy holidays. The buses were waiting so John and Rachel marched the kids away.

Time off. Dez sighed with delight. She and Leo strolled to the building.

He held the door for her. "Can you leave for the day? Or do you need to talk with the cops or something?"

"I can leave. I gave Jason a...a statement he called it. He said he'd let me know if they had more questions. Do you have to stay longer?"

"I'll come back later after the cops are done. How about going out for a coffee or something?"

Dez shook her head.

His walk slowed. "Oh."

Dez slipped her hand in his. "Maybe you could come over to my place? I have leftovers and some great music to listen to."

That brought back a spring to his step. "Hang on just a minute. I'll grab my stuff." Dez leaned into the maintenance doorway. He said, "Looks like the cops came and took the computer." He opened his locker and grabbed a bag. "Okay, let's go."

She pointed to the decorated bag. "What's that?"

"Actually, it's a surprise for you." He held up a bag of Snow Kiss Cookies. "They're fresh from Sandy's bakery."

She faced him. "You saved my life. Jason told me about it. You saved my life. Like William and Emma."

He brushed back a lock of her hair from her face. "These cookies are the real thing." He opened the bag. "They have powdered sugar."

She took one out and looked at the generous powdered sugar on top. "They sure do." She waved one in front of Leo. "Want a taste?"

He took an enthusiastic bite.

She laughed to see the powder stuck to his lips. She took a bite too.

He gave her his mischievous grin. "Forelsket."